'No fiancé

'No fiancé,' [...]
meaning to talk [...]

She gathered [...]
looked into the [...]ness of his eyes. 'I said I'd
go ahead—have an affair with you—and I'm
okay with that. But I think we should establish
some ground rules first.'

Good, she'd managed to startle him, by the
look of things.

'Ground rules?' The words growled into the
air between them.

'Yes,' Kirsten told him, standing straighter as
her confidence built. 'Parameters—that kind
of thing. For a start, I'd like to know how long
your affairs usually last. Are we talking a
month? Six weeks?'

Startled didn't begin to describe his expression now. Stunned came close.

'I thought we should put some kind of time
limit on it. I'm not up on flings, but *you* must
know how long your affairs usually last.'

'I haven't actually, consciously, timed my past
affairs,' Josh said, attempting, with difficulty,
to keep the growl out of his voice.

Dear Reader

Over the last few years I've really enjoyed reading 'relationship' books involving the lives of young, single career women juggling priorities to find enough time for love, friendship, shopping and even basic personal maintenance. Generally, the support network of other single friends keeps them sane, so the idea of helping four friends find love really appealed to me.

Gabi, Kirsten, Alana and Daisy all live in the Near West apartment building, and work or have worked at the Royal Westside Hospital. Gabi, a doctor, has loved and lost. Kirsten, an occupational therapist, has been held in the grip of unrequited love. Nurse Alana's previous venture into romance has left her preferring the company of her pets; though she strongly believes in love, she theorises that it grows from friendship, not attraction. Daisy is a psychologist who can tell them why things happen as they do, but can't quite sort out her own problems.

The four friends share each other's tears and laughter, and, often with unexpected consequences, try to help each other along the rocky road to love.

I have had such fun getting to know these women as I wrote these four books, and I hope you enjoy their company as much as I have.

Meredith Webber

Look out for the next two WESTSIDE STORIES:

THE DOCTOR'S DESTINY (Alana's story)
DAISY AND THE DOCTOR (Daisy's story)

Coming soon from Mills & Boon® Medical Romance™

Recent titles by the same author:

DR GRAHAM'S MARRIAGE (Gabi's story)
CHRISTMAS KNIGHT
THE MARRIAGE GAMBLE

DEAR
DOCTOR

BY
MEREDITH WEBBER

MILLS & BOON®

First published in Great Britain 2002
Harlequin Mills & Boon Limited,
Eton House, 18-24 Paradise Road, Richmond, Surrey TW9 1SR

© Meredith Webber 2002

ISBN 0 263 83424 7

Set in Times Roman 10½ on 12 pt.
03-0203-48850

Printed and bound in Spain
by Litografía Rosés, S.A., Barcelona

CHAPTER ONE

Too keyed up to wait for the lift, Kirsten raced up the stairs of the apartment building, Near West, paused momentarily in the fourth-floor foyer to catch her breath, then, still fizzing with excitement, gave a perfunctory tap on Gabi's door, flung it open and with the 'Ta da!' cry of an impending announcement flashed her left hand towards her startled friend.

And her startled friend's equally startled new—and former—husband.

Husband! Damn it all! In all the excitement she'd forgotten.

Again!

'Oh, Alex, I'm sorry! I've got to get over doing this, haven't I? Dashing in uninvited like I used to do before you came back. You two could have been up to anything!'

She smiled winsomely at Alex.

'Forgive me? Just this once? After all, we're about to become related.'

'Related?' Alex echoed, shaking his head. He'd been acquainted with Kirsten, who lived in the flat opposite theirs on the fourth floor, for more than three months now, and thought he'd mastered the art of following her ditzy and often extremely convoluted conversations, but this one had him stumped.

'You and Grant? You're engaged?' Ha! Gabi had rescued him. Kirsten had met Gabi's brother at his and Gabi's second wedding—but engaged? When the wedding was only a week ago?

He shook his head, pleased Gabi seemed to be handling the situation for both of them. She was holding Kirsten's left hand, looking at the magnificent diamond that sparkled on the ring finger.

'I drove him to the airport this morning so he could fly back to that never-never world your family inhabit, and just before he walked over to his little plane, he gave me this. It was such a surprise. I mean, we haven't slept together or anything. Well, you know I don't, Gabi, not with someone I've just met. Not for at least a month, that's my rule.'

Alex struggled to make sense of someone who wouldn't sleep with a man for a month because she didn't know him well enough, but would commit to marry someone she'd known a whole week. Because that's all the time Grant had had in the city.

And from the patently false smile on Gabi's face, she had some misgivings as well. Though when she voiced them it wasn't her brother's welfare she was considering.

'What about Josh?' she asked—blunt as only Gabi could be blunt. Was she talking about Josh Phillips, the man Alex was certain had been hanging around Gabi only a few months ago?

Alex watched a little of the sparkle fade from Kirsten's lovely green eyes, and imagined the glow which lit her skin had also diminished slightly.

'He doesn't give a damn about me, Gabi, and never will. He's all hooked up on this marrying late thing, and he had the hide to use my age as an excuse—why keep me hanging around through all my best child-bearing years? No, Josh will wait until he's forty then take a young trophy bride to bear beautiful babies. She'll stay at home to look after them, and cook him wonderful meals and entertain the right people, and never make an exhibition of herself splitting her skirt to the thigh while getting out of his car on the way to a specialists' dinner.'

'But I thought you'd been seeing him again recently?' Gabi said, while Alex struggled with an impulse to ask about the split skirt—and the reaction of the specialists at dinner!

Kirsten sighed.

'Not *that* recently!' she admitted. 'It was back when Alex first returned from Scotland. Josh came around a few times and my silly heart did its flip-flop thing, but all he wanted to talk about was you and Alex, and how to get the Grahams back together again.'

And though securely remarried to his ex-wife, and confident in their mutual love, Alex still felt a tiny spurt of relief at this explanation of Josh's car having been parked outside the building. At the time, he'd suffered agonies of jealousy but had never questioned Gabi about it, and had tucked the matter away once they'd been reconciled. But, hey, he was only a man, and jealousy was practically obligatory in the male psyche.

Kirsten had switched the subject back to Grant, how wonderful he was, how kind, considerate, warm, funny, understanding, and most of all, dedicated to commitment.

Alex sensed it was only with difficulty that Gabi wasn't rolling her eyes, particularly at the last description. Which did seem a trifle over-optimistic. Alex's knowledge of Grant was from visits to the family property when Grant was always working, and his not infrequent sorties to the city, flying in for wool sales, or to pick out a stud bull at the big agricultural show. At these times there'd usually been an attractive woman attached to his admittedly well-muscled arm.

But Gabi, bless her soft romantic heart, was saying all

the right things, hugging Kirsten and wishing her well.
Offering coffee.

'No! Grant and I have been up all night—just talking
and talking. There's been so little time and he won't be
able to get down until after the shearing and crutching.'

Kirsten sent a puzzled smile at Gabi.

'I didn't want to show the full extent of my ignorance
in front of Grant, but what exactly is crutching?'

Alex hid a smile as Gabi explained, and Kirsten's 'Oh,
gross!' came right on cue.

'At least you'll have the challenge of working out what
perfume works best at such times,' Alex teased, remembering the nose-numbing task he'd once had, sniffing his
way through Kirsten's forty-seven different perfumes in
an effort to establish for her what worked best for men.

'Oh, I won't have to bother about that any more,'
Kirsten said blithely. 'Grant really doesn't like perfume
and he says it upsets the dogs when they're working, so
I'll give it up.'

Gabi was now looking seriously worried, and Alex put
his arm around her shoulders to give her a hug of silent
support.

Then Kirsten added, 'What kind of work do the dogs
actually do? Do they track the sheep, that perfume might
upset them?'

Gabi's shoulders relaxed as the question broke her up
completely.

It was minutes before she had her chuckles finally under control, and she mopped at her streaming eyes, kissed
Kirsten on the cheek and said, 'I can see I'll have to give
you some lessons before you actually head west to the
property.'

Alex expected Kirsten to object to Gabi's mirth, but he
realised she was thinking even further ahead when she

nodded seriously, then added, 'And come shopping with me so I know what to buy—I know city clothes won't do at all.'

And on that happy note—he'd learnt that shopping always made Kirsten happy—she departed, heading for bed, no doubt to make up for the many nights of sleep she'd missed while Grant had been in town.

'Well?' Alex asked Gabi, when he was sure Kirsten was unlikely to return.

Gabi shook her head.

'It might work out—who knows? I know Grant's always been a love-'em-and-leave-'em type but he's never given anyone an engagement ring before.'

She sighed.

'Well, not that I know of!'

She was looking so concerned Alex felt obliged to kiss her, and that led to other pleasurable things, though he did remember to lock the front door before heading to the bedroom. Gabi's open-door policy had led to other embarrassing moments since his return. And on Saturday morning, a number of the building's mostly medical inhabitants would be off duty. Who knew who might walk in next?

Kirsten managed to sleep through most of the weekend so by Monday morning, when she reported for work, she was refreshed but still high with excitement, particularly as Grant was proving the most exemplary fiancé, phoning each evening to tell her how much he missed her, how much he loved her and how the shearing and crutching was progressing. She could have lived without the crutching details, which made intimate bits of her anatomy squirm in discomfort, but shearing was OK. After all, lightweight wool was now used by the best designers for some stunning creations.

Aware that the rock on her finger would attract attention and comment, she dressed with particular care—which involved trying on fourteen combinations of clothes before settling on the one she'd tried on fourth—and seventh, and tenth. It was a knee-length straight skirt in a caramel-coloured, stretchy material, and it fitted her like a second skin. On top she wore a caramel and white knit top with enough splashes of green in the pattern to highlight her eyes.

'So, the newly engaged woman sallies forth to work!' her friend Alana teased when she joined Kirsten in the foyer of the building as both were setting out for work. Health freak Alana had, of course, used the stairs.

She'd also, over the weekend, inspected the ring, so Kirsten sought approval for her outfit and received assurances that it hit just the right note.

'Engaged but efficient!' Alana said, and Kirsten tried to see if she was hiding a smile as she said it, but as there didn't seem to be any merriment in Alana's eyes, she accepted the words as a compliment.

One she needed for boosting her morale when she arrived in the occupational therapy department, just a little late because so many people had noticed the ring and stopped to congratulate her, and was told Josh Phillips had been asking for her.

'He's phoned three times,' Clare, the Occupational Therapy department secretary, told her. 'Might be something to do with the new unit they're setting up down in the kids' ward.'

'New unit? I've only been away a fortnight, not a year. What new unit?'

Clare's offhand shrug made Kirsten want to shake her.

The secretaries knew more about what went on in the hospital than anyone, with the possible exception of the cleaners.

Though from some of the things cleaners had told her, she thought they probably made up a lot of it.

'So, does he want to see me?' Kirsten asked, when it was obvious Clare wasn't going to answer the unit question.

'I don't know,' Clare replied. 'He just kept phoning, kept asking to speak to you, and I kept saying you weren't here.' The phone rang, and she added, 'This might be him now,' before lifting the receiver and positively cooing a hello.

'Oh, it's you, Marie.' The cooing stopped. 'Yes, I went last night. You've no idea...'

Kirsten moved away, no wiser about why Josh might want to speak to her, or about the new unit, but definitely not wanting to hear the intimate details of Clare's social life.

But as she stowed her handbag in her locker, and tried to decide whether to stay in her gorgeous green sandals or change into sensible flats, an image of Josh Phillips flitted through her head. Hopefully, he had nothing to do with her decision to keep the sandals on, because she was, after all, over him. And engaged. Though, now she thought about it, she'd bought them the first time he'd asked her out, and had worn them several times during that whirlwind month when the attraction between them had been so strong, she'd almost broken her rule...

She sighed, then breathed on the diamond on the third finger of her left hand and rubbed the stone against her skirt.

No, keeping the sandals on was a reasonable decision based on the fact she was scheduled to do desk work today, working out the rotation for the students who'd be coming into the hospital for four weeks practical work next week, before university started again in late February. Each student needed a mentor, so that had to be sorted out as well. And once that was done, there were work schedules and a tutorial to prepare…

She crossed to the pigeonholes on the far side of the room, pulled out all the papers from her own, then dumped the lot on the desk all the OTs used from time to time. She was putting hospital circulars into one heap and OT news into another when the phone rang.

Clare was still regaling Marie with the details of her weekend and obviously had no intention of cutting short her conversation to take a work-related call, so it had switched automatically through to the phone on the second desk.

You're over Josh, Kirsten reminded herself as she reached out to pick up the receiver. You're engaged to a hunky country man who just adores you and, better still, is ready to settle down, she lectured herself as her fingers hesitated above the moulded plastic receiver.

'Yes?'

'Are you always this late for work?'

Not only over him but wondering what she'd ever seen in him, the rude, arrogant beast!

'Is that relevant to whatever you want to know?' she snapped, as much disturbed by a silly hangover-type weakness in her knees as by his attitude.

'I don't suppose so,' he replied, super-cool—but, then, he always was. All the Phillips men were cool—they probably had cool bred into them along with the genes that made them all doctors. Past and present members of the Phillips family formed a hierarchy so entrenched within the hospital and the medical world beyond it that they were spoken of with the awe usually reserved for royalty.

'Well?' Kirsten demanded, when she realised from the silence it might be her turn to talk, then found she didn't have anything to say. Apart from 'I'm wearing the sandals I bought to go out with you', and that didn't seem appropriate.

Particularly when he was already breathing fire.

'I wanted to speak to you about something, but it's too late now. I've an appointment in five minutes, then I'll be on the run all morning. Perhaps lunchtime? Twelve-thirty looks good for me. Coffee-shop or canteen?'

She must have mumbled something he thought he understood, for after an abrupt 'Good, twelve-thirty in the coffee-shop, I'll see you then', he hung up.

Kirsten turned the receiver towards her and stared at it.

Had she really just had that weird conversation with Josh Phillips?

She looked across at Clare who'd apparently finished her conversation with Marie and was now buffing her nails.

'What new unit?' Kirsten asked her, then she frowned as ferociously as she could. 'And don't tell me you don't know.'

Clare did her shrugging thing again, and pouted petulantly.

'It's for kids with leukaemia—and maybe one of the anaemias, but mainly leukaemia. They're setting up for transplants of some kind. I don't know why it's such a big deal. Marion was asked to suggest an OT and she suggested you and Dr Phillips said he thought Dorothy would be better, or Candace, or maybe we should advertise.'

Kirsten listened to this explanation with growing disbelief. Marion, head of the OT department, had suggested her, Kirsten Collins, and Josh had turned her down! For the transplant unit for which she had personally raised a lot of money but which they'd all thought had been a long-term dream?

Disbelief and anger warred, and though she knew anger would win, she didn't want to unleash it yet. No! Just keep it simmering nicely along until twelve-thirty—or would she make that twelve thirty-five?

In the end she decided punctuality would suit her best, but even so, when she entered the coffee-shop at exactly twelve-thirty, he was already there. She paused just inside the door, pleased to get the initial 'seeing Josh' reactions out of the way. Studied him, wondering why one man—handsome enough but not startlingly so—could produce physical symptoms in her body when she worked with men as good-looking, well-built and far more charismatic every day.

It was all to do with sex appeal, and neither her studies nor any amount of 'answer yes or no' in the pop psychology quizzes she loved doing had ever satisfactorily explained exactly what that was.

But forget sex appeal, she was here for business—and, if necessary, blood!

Josh Phillips's blood!

Thus girded for battle, Kirsten strode past the scatter of people queued at the counter as they waited to order, and approached her prey. She waited until she was right beside the table, then she leaned forward and said, 'Now, before I bother to sit down, am I in or out of the new unit?'

Good! At least he had the grace to look startled, though he'd have had to be brain dead not to guess she'd hear about it some time this morning.

'What do you mean, in or out?' he said, recovering well, the rat! He even had the cheek to smile, before adding in his best conciliatory tone, 'Look, why don't you sit down? I've arranged for Mavis to take our order from the table as soon as we're both seated. Saves a bit of time that way.'

The statement added fuel to Kirsten's burning sense of injustice. A lesser person would have grown cobwebs waiting for table service in this coffee-shop—but not Josh!

Though it might be worth relenting enough to sit for the sheer pleasure of being waited on by cranky Mavis.

Kirsten slid into the seat, then realised it was a mistake. The tables were so small her knees were practically brushing his, and now she was on a level with him there was the added disadvantage of having to look into his eyes. Eyes so blue, so direct, so…tactile somehow they should have been registered as lethal weapons.

'Well?' she demanded, then realised she'd tried that demand earlier in the day and had got nowhere.

Neither was she going to get anywhere with it now, or not immediately, because Mavis had, true to Josh's word, suddenly materialised by their sides and was smiling dotingly at the paediatrician.

'She's known me since I was a kid,' Josh said, when she'd taken their order and departed. 'I'd occasionally come in to the hospital with my father on weekends. We took turns, the three of us boys. I think it was the only bonding thing he ever did with his sons—drive to the hospital with one of us every week. Anyway, he'd drop me off in the coffee-shop. Mavis would make me pink lemonade and a banana split and keep an eye on me while he did his rounds.'

'A little treat for the crown prince?' Kirsten said, and saw surprise flicker in Josh's eyes.

'I don't think we ever saw ourselves as anything special,' he protested. 'Or see ourselves as special now.'

Kirsten laughed.

'No? When every day you walk past Phillips Ward, Phillips Lecture Room, the Phillips Family Withdrawing Suite?'

Josh looked uncomfortable, which, as far as Kirsten was concerned, was just fine. Why should she be the only one suffering?

And what had happened to her anger? Surely simply sitting opposite him hadn't been enough to douse it?

No, a lot had been dispelled by one telling sentence he'd let slip, and though she'd made light of his confession, teasing him about the family, the remark about the only bonding thing his father had ever done had jabbed through her defences. For a moment there, she'd felt almost sorry for him.

Rebuilding time. This was not a man one faced with weakened defences!

She thought about the unit and felt her anger flare again.

Good!

'So, what about this unit? Is it what you wanted to discuss? Are you offering me a job in it or not?'

Again he looked uncomfortable—as well he might if what Clare had said was true!

'Kirsten…' he began, his voice tailing off in a most un-Josh-like manner. This was a man with the confidence to reduce sloppy junior staff to tears in two minutes flat and, not five minutes later, win them back to smiling sycophancy. 'It's not that I don't think you'd—'

Mavis returned, and as Kirsten lifted her hand to take

the plate the waitress held out to her, Josh saw the flash of light from the rock-size stone in a ring on the third finger of her left hand.

Kirsten was engaged?

Panic rushed through him, though it should have been relief.

He tried the thought again, only this time with a different spin.

Kirsten was engaged, full stop, finito, that's it.

Much better!

And engaged people usually got married sooner rather than later, which gave him an out as far as employing her on the unit was concerned.

So why did he feel as if he'd suddenly developed a perforated ulcer?

He glanced across the table, wondering why she wasn't questioning the silence, saw the heavy fall of red-brown hair, the creamy, lightly freckled skin.

'Don't mess with redheads—they're flighty, capricious, and usually bad-tempered' had been practically the only father-son advice his father had ever given him. Actually, his father had probably said 'don't get involved with' rather than 'mess with', but the implication had been there. His father hadn't followed up the statement with any illustrations of this warning, but just in case, for the month when Josh had been engaged in a preliminary skirmish with this particular redhead, he'd kept telling himself her hair was more brown than red, really.

Really!

It just looked red today. And the green eyes made you think red hair.

He couldn't see the cool green eyes because she was totally absorbed in investigating the contents of her bowl of salad, picking through it with her fork as if counting the individual pieces. He had a silly urge to smile, because it was *so* Kirsten! No matter what the situation, food should be considered seriously.

Though possibly not as seriously as clothes.

He hauled his mind back to the subject they were supposedly discussing.

'As far as the unit is concerned, I wanted people on the team willing to commit to it on an ongoing basis. I know you were there in the beginning, and did a lot of the initial fund-raising work, but you moved on from the paediatric ward, so I assumed you wouldn't be interested in the unit. Now, by the look of things, you're heading for a new stage of your life. Are congratulations in order?'

There, that had worked well. He was sufficiently satisfied with this lucid summing-up to take a bite of his steak sandwich, only to choke on it when she said, 'I'd have thought you'd be more likely to offer commiserations to the man involved. After all, a man who turns pale and sweaty at the thought of commitment must have some fellow-feeling for the ring-giver.'

'I don't think any of this is relevant,' Josh said, and heard the stiffness of anger echoing back to him from his own words.

'Of course it isn't,' she snapped right back at him. 'What's relevant is choosing the best people for the job. I assume that's why you asked Marion for her recommendation. So why turn it down? Turn *me* down when she recommended me.'

'I was concerned about your commitment.' Damn, there was that word again. 'After all, you moved on from Paediatrics rather suddenly, and I didn't want that happening again. You took leave, if I remember.'

Which, at the time, had angered him because, instead of being relieved that he hadn't had to see her somewhere on the ward every day, he'd found himself missing her vibrant presence—looking for her when he'd known she was no longer there.

And repeating over and over to himself his father's advice!

'And now you're engaged—'

The emerald eyes narrowed.

'Let's keep my private life out of this,' she said. 'Though I distinctly remember telling you that I intended working at least part time after marriage. I think it went on to the long list of reasons why I wasn't a suitable partner for a Phillips. Oh, I know you didn't mention suitability—you stuck with the 'not ready for commitment' excuse—but it was there all the time, wasn't it, Josh? There in the back of your mind. There when you'd take me out to dinner but took Roberta Smythe to the hospital ball in case I didn't fit in with the rest of the Phillips clan.'

'I explained that to you, Kirsten. It was a long-standing arrangement.'

But he was shocked by her perception. He hadn't consciously thought about how she might fit into his formidable family—and if he had, his concern would have been for her. For her comfort in their presence.

But his decision to be honest with her—to tell her, before it even properly began, that it would only be an affair and have no future—*had* probably had something to do with the fact that she certainly didn't fit the image of the woman he had always thought he might, eventually, marry. A woman who would be content to be a consort rather than a wife—who would understand he had responsibilities to his work, and the hospital, and not expect or demand too much of his time and attention.

No, he couldn't see vibrant, colourful, beautiful Kirsten

in that role. She might not demand attention—almost certainly wouldn't, for she was supremely self-sufficient—but that wouldn't stop him being driven to distraction wondering what she was up to every moment he wasn't with her.

In fact, he'd started to see what his father had meant...

'I don't know why we're discussing this anyway,' Josh said, his own discomfort making him speak more sharply than he'd intended. 'What's past is past. As far as the unit is concerned, I wanted an OT who could take a wider role. We've got to consider the implications of the long-term hospitalisation of patients, and the effect of this on them and their families. Bone-marrow and stem-cell transplants are usually the "last chance" for these kids, and although there are social workers available to the parents, I don't have the funds to have a counsellor full time on the unit.'

'But the OT is there and usually available to speak to parents so you thought you might be able to find an OT with some counselling training or experience?' Kirsten guessed, then her eyes narrowed and he knew he wasn't going to like what came next. 'Like Dorothy, who did a psych degree before her OT—or perhaps me, who did psychology for my masters, and included studies on the effects of long-term hospitalisation in children?'

'You've got a masters? In psychology?'

He couldn't have sounded more surprised if she'd told him she had three legs and a tail. Then surprise turned to suspicion. Kirsten saw it flare in the blue eyes before he shot the question at her.

'Why?'

'Why do a master's? Because I like studying. No, that's not true. Like most people, I hate studying, but I like learning things, knowing things. I dithered along, doing various subjects part time for years after I finished my OT, then I decided to get serious, applied to do the further degree. When I was accepted, I streamlined my studies and finally took some leave last year to complete it. Why psychology?'

She grinned at him.

'It seemed as good a way as any to find out how men tick.'

She turned her attention back to her salad, knowing full well she'd confused him—and delighted by this small victory. What she didn't tell him was that taking time off to complete her master's had got her away from the hospital and the risk of running into him, while studying had filled in the empty hours. It had been her panacea for heartbreak.

'And did you?'

She glanced up, a black olive arrested halfway to her lips while she thought back to work out what he was asking.

'Find out how men ticked?' she guessed.

He wasn't smiling and, as far as she could tell, there was no humour in the words, or lurking around his luscious lips, or sparkling in those killer eyes.

'Some men,' she said carefully, then she lifted the olive and bit down on its saltiness, wondering just how bluntly she could get the conversation off this strange byway and back to discussion of the unit.

'Yet you still work as an occupational therapist?' Relief! He'd done it for her. 'Surely with a second degree, working in some kind of counselling or psychotherapy role would be more—'

'Remunerative?'

Josh seemed taken aback by her interjection, and she stole the moment to add, 'Money isn't everything, is it?

Working with children has always been my favourite thing. But any hospital work, particularly work in a cancer ward where I do so much distraction therapy, involves contact with a lot of grief, a lot of stress, a lot of despair. I wanted—no, make that needed—to learn how to handle it myself, and hopefully be able to offer help to others. As well as that, I'd done Psych I and II in my OT training, then did a third unit as an optional in my final year, so following it up was a natural progression.'

'But you haven't been working with children. You've been working with stroke victims,' he reminded her, seizing on the weakness in her argument which she'd tried to cover with talk of the degree.

Was he hoping she'd admit she'd avoided Paediatrics on her return because of him?

If so, he'd be disappointed. No way was she going there.

'Stroke victims have a lot of psychological adjusting to do as well,' she reminded him. 'But we've got a long way off this unit, haven't we? And if I'm not being offered a position on it, why did you want to see me?'

He'd gone beyond taken aback this time. Downright shocked, that's how he looked. She'd snapped the questions at him, mainly to avoid any further discussion of why she wasn't working with children right now.

'I wanted to tell you personally,' he began, and Kirsten, as her anger reached simmering point again, finished for him.

'Tell me personally why you didn't choose me for it? Explain why, when I helped with the initial fund-raising and had discussed it with you so often, you didn't think I'd be suitable? OK, come on, tell me. Say it outright. Say, "I don't want you, Kirsten."'

He stopped pretending to eat, put down his sandwich,

wiped his fingers, then reached across the table to, oh, so lightly brush a touch across her left hand.

'Ah, but I do, you see,' he murmured, his husky voice sending vibes right through Kirsten's body. 'That's part of the problem. I'm still attracted to you, Kirsten. That's never changed.'

CHAPTER TWO

IT TOOK a moment for the words to make sense, then another for Kirsten to take in the full import of it.

Blow the vibes—she couldn't put up with this!

'Are you expecting me to believe you'd be so unprofessional as to let a little thing like lust influence your decision on the choice of personnel for the unit? You, the great Josh Phillips, admitting your...' suddenly aware of where she was, she hauled back the colourful word that had nearly popped out of her mouth and made a quick substitution '...libido rules your brains?'

The blue gaze narrowed, and his lips thinned.

'You're the one who made a precipitate departure from the paediatric ward when our relationship, such as it was, ended.'

The reminder showed he'd known all along why she'd left, so when he'd asked earlier, his sole purpose had been an attempt to get her to admit it. Well, she wasn't going to—not now and not ever.

She smiled as sweetly as she could, and, ignoring the various degrees of heat just being near him still caused, said, with carefully manufactured aplomb, 'Ah, but that was all before I'd met Grant.'

She waggled her left hand in case she needed to underline the message, then said, 'Now, about the job.'

Josh was saved by his pager—vibrating with an urgent summons to the paediatric ward.

'Don't worry about the bill. Mavis will put it on my tab.' He stood up and dropped his serviette beside his unfinished sandwich, and made a quick decision. 'There's a meeting of unit staff in Room 63 at nine tomorrow morning. Nine sharp. I'll see you there.'

The surprise on Kirsten's face gave him some satisfaction, but not enough to wipe away the gnawing anxiety in his gut.

She *was* the best person for the job, he reminded himself as he walked away. She had been even before he'd known about her second degree. *He'd* known it before Marion, head of the OT department, had mentioned her, and Kirsten knew he knew it. And, as she'd pointed out, she was engaged, which surely should make a difference to how he felt about her.

Problem was, it didn't seem to be damping down the attraction that had always flared when he was near her, though perhaps, once he got used to the idea that she was no longer available, this would happen.

Not that she'd ever been *that* available. In the beginning, though attracted to her from the moment he'd first seen her, he'd avoided asking her out. Even ignoring the redhead thing, she'd come across as someone who just wanted to have fun, while his preferred date was a serious, intelligent woman who had more on her mind than clothes and social outings. But they had been thrown together on the ward, and he'd admired the way she could think beyond the sometimes narrow parameters of hospital work. Then a child had died, a child they'd both found special, and they'd begun to talk of the possibility of having a transplant unit.

Her enthusiasm hadn't let it stop at talk, and she'd bullied him into starting on a submission, then she'd set up a fund-raising committee, so they'd seen more of each other outside working hours. And he'd realised how misleading first impressions could be. Beneath the outrageously trendy exterior, there was a woman who went after what she wanted, dragging laggards in her wake.

When he'd eventually given in to the attraction and asked her out—on a date, as distinct from a talk about work over dinner—he'd assumed it would lead to a mutually pleasurable relationship which would, in due time, run its course. They would then part, with no pain or recriminations on either side, probably remaining friends.

It's how things happened with him, and it seemed to work for the women he dated, most of whom drifted out of his life once they realised his commitment to his job left him little time for anything else. Including them.

'Hi, Dr Phillips.'

A pert blonde stepped into the lift beside him. The new resident from the children's orthopaedic ward. Betty? Beryl?

'Bella Rossiter,' she said, as if sensing his struggle.

Josh smiled at her, and recognised the gleam of interest in her sparkling brown eyes, but he was still picturing eyes the colour of emeralds—or were they more like clear, deep, creek water on hot summer days?

Nothing had gone right with Kirsten. Nothing! For a start, there had been her ridiculous embargo on sex for the first month of a relationship, and the challenge of trying to break her down had nearly wrecked him. Then, bang, right when he'd known for sure he'd finally got somewhere—in fact, when they'd both been naked in his bedroom—some ridiculous notion of chivalry had forced him to admit that, for the moment, he wasn't looking for a long-term relationship, and that their affair, while no doubt it would be totally pleasurable, would not lead to any permanent commitment.

He could still see her, first leaving the bed with the swift movement of a gazelle in flight, then the beautiful breasts falling forward as she'd pulled on the scanty wisp of lace that passed for panties.

More amused than concerned, at that stage, he'd watched her performance.

'Sudden change of heart? No longer interested?' he said jokingly—sure he could redeem matters because a certain part of his body definitely *hadn't* lost interest. In fact, if anything, it seemed more interested as she encased those beautiful breasts in another, matching scrap of lace.

'I don't think I'm fling material,' she said, as calmly as she might have mentioned her star sign. She was pulling on her skirt by then, straightening it with what seemed to be unsteady hands. He could remember thinking unsteady might be a hopeful sign. 'I have no doubt an affair with you would be wonderful, but it would also be self-indulgent because it would be nothing more than physical pleasure-seeking.'

'So, what are you saying?' he demanded, finally realising she was serious. 'It's marriage or nothing—is that it?'

'No!' Indignation propelled the word out of her mouth with the velocity of a rifle shot. 'Of course I don't want that. I just can't come to terms with a relationship that has limits on it—that doesn't hold the open-ended excitement of what might develop between us. To me, the whole affair would be stunted from the start—like a bonsai tree, unable to grow past a certain stage of development because its roots have been hacked off. So why bother?'

And with that, and with the gorgeous breast-laden bra now decently covered, she walked out of his apartment and within days disappeared from the hospital.

Worse still, she also disappeared off the fund-raising committee. Her excuse for dropping out of that, now he thought back, *had* been something to do with study commitments. An excuse he'd totally dismissed at the time.

Kirsten studying? What?

Fashion co-ordination?

Even though he'd known her better by then, a master's degree in psychology wouldn't have been his next guess—or the one after that!

Then, some time later, she'd been back—not in Paediatrics but back in the hospital, so, with Sod's law working well, he had been forever running into her, or coming upon her unexpectedly.

She was like a planet, glitteringly bright, effortlessly attracting attention, zooming across the skies, but plotting her own erratic course—not following any rules a man could understand. And it was that very unpredictability that made her dangerous—and totally unsuitable for any long-term relationship, though he wasn't ready to consider that with anyone just yet.

He refused to accept her behaviour could have had anything to do with her hair colour, though from time to time he had wondered...

'You've not heard a word I've said.'

Startled by the comment, he glanced around and caught Bella's amused smile.

'It wasn't important,' she told him. 'Just asking if you were going to the Bush Dance to celebrate Australia Day—the money's going to your new unit, isn't it?'

He pulled himself together, smiled at Bella and admitted that, yes, he'd be at the dance.

With gritted teeth! he added silently because he hated that kind of socialising, while as for dressing up...

But as well as raising money, the special unit committee raised awareness of the need for people to register as bone-marrow donors, and as donors were desperately needed, he had no choice but to be present.

How you look should be the last thing bothering you, Kirsten told herself as she hurried, determined not to be a minute late, to Room 63. Anyway, you look fine. Didn't Alex remark what a great outfit it was as we all walked to work?

'Tell that to your knees,' she muttered, the mad internal dialogue continuing as she pushed open the door to the small lecture room.

Josh was sorting papers at a table at the front of the room, but perhaps the door opening distracted him, for he glanced up and for a fleeting instant a smile of such delight lit his face that Kirsten's knees became the least of her problems.

Then his expression sobered and he nodded to her, saying, 'Kirsten, thanks for coming. Take a seat and I'll introduce you when the rest get here.'

Kirsten found a seat—which was good as far as the boneless legs were concerned—but that fleeting smile had destroyed what little composure she'd managed to rustle up. Drawing in a deep breath, she set her functioning neurones to work on reminders of her status as a fiancée.

Someone else's fiancée.

Seeking distraction, she turned to the woman beside her, an older woman she recognised from her time in the paediatric wards.

'Betty, isn't it? I'm Kirsten Collins.'

'The OT,' Betty said, holding out her hand to Kirsten. 'I wasn't there long before you left, but I know the kids loved you working with them. They really missed you when you left. I heard you were back at the hospital—where have you been working?'

'Strokes!' Kirsten shuddered as she spoke. Though she knew the work she did with stroke victims was essential for their recovery and long-term ability to function, she still hated seeing the once-active people so debilitated by the terrible trauma.

'Well, that was a change!' Betty said, and Kirsten wasn't able to resist glancing towards Josh, who continued sorting through his papers. Maybe she should have stuck it out, even though working with and near him had become a personal hell. Maybe if she had, the effect he had on her would have lessened over time, and by now she'd have been able to look at him without the slightest bone weakness or tremor of desire.

He looked up and her heart did a little tap-dance, but she knew that was simply habit on its part. Wasn't she safely engaged to Grant, who was just the most wonderful man in the entire world?

And committed!

More people entered the room, shuffled into seats, then looked expectantly towards Josh. He'd finished sorting papers and was now writing what seemed to be voluminous notes. It gave Kirsten time to study him. Not that she didn't know exactly what he looked like, so it was more a consideration of why this one man affected her as he did.

Had affected her!

He wasn't drop-dead handsome. In fact, compared to other men she'd been out with, he was way down the list of good-lookers, while put up against Grant he was almost ordinary.

For a start, there was that thatch of straight, dark brown hair which stuck up at all angles as the day wore on and he thrust his fingers through it more and more often. When first cut, it looked great, but as he was always rushing around the place, barber appointments weren't top of his priority list.

Good brow, wide and high, but no exaggerations, and the hard slashes of his cheekbones—well, they were something else, protruding far enough to leave interestingly shadowed hollows beneath them, giving him that slightly worn and hungry look that led women to want to care for him.

Safer to care for a full-grown grizzly! Kirsten reminded herself, then returned to her cataloguing of his features.

His nose was good—it was straight and in the right place with no deviations or hooks or bumps or other startlingly offputting features. And his lips, right beneath that nose, well, she had to admit they were so, well, right somehow—they were almost indescribable. Full but not too full for a man, and mobile, smiling easily, though often that smile held a hint of mockery. While their expertise on the kissing front...

A little tremor started in her chest at the thought of Josh's kisses, but with the new-found confidence of a woman wearing an engagement ring, she reminded herself that Grant was no slouch in the kissing department, while the way he trailed his fingers along the slope of her shoulder...

'Kirsten!'

The sound of her name—on Josh's lips—brought her out of her memories of Grant. Looking up, she met the feature she'd been avoiding—again—in her impartial consideration of Josh's face—the blue, blue eyes. Neither light nor dark, but vivid in a way she'd thought only contact-lens-enhanced eyes could ever be. Though Josh's eye colour was the real thing...

'Are you with us? I'm introducing you all. This is

Kirsten Collins, an occupational therapist who has had considerable experience in the paediatric ward.'

He moved on to introduce Betty, and Kirsten looked around. Presumably, those who'd been listening to the introductions now knew who was who, and, without doubt, they all knew why they were there.

She turned back to Josh and sensed an excitement radiating from him—saw it shining in those mesmerising eyes.

'Well, now you all know each other, we can get on with the business,' he said. 'I'm sure all of you already know that funding has finally been approved for a special unit within the paediatric department for stem-cell and bone-marrow transplantation. Until now, children under our care who needed this type of service had to go onto a waiting list for the procedure to be done at the Children's Hospital.'

Kirsten caught the nod from Josh, a reminder of when they'd first become close—when a young patient, dear to both of them, had died while on that waiting list.

At the time, they'd talked for hours about getting more facilities so the waiting time could be reduced. Bad enough that donor material wasn't always available, but to have a donor and not have the facilities to do the retrieval and transplant—that had struck Kirsten as criminal. She'd said so to Josh and had helped him prepare a submission—started a fund-raising committee. It was where they'd first got to know each other as people rather than as fellow professionals.

And to think he'd even *consider* not appointing her to the team! The temper she swore had nothing to do with reddish-coloured hair fizzed inside her but she forced herself to concentrate on the rest of the presentation.

'I've selected you people for the team who will work

in this unit. You're my wish list. Some of you may opt not to take a position in it, but I was told I could choose my team, and I wanted the best. As far as I'm concerned, you *are* the best.'

Well, the rest might be, but you sure had doubts about me, Kirsten wanted to remind him.

'Catherine, for example,' Josh continued, indicating a woman in the front row, 'was instrumental in getting the cord blood bank started here at Royal Westside, and while we won't be the only unit after precious stem cells from umbilical cord blood, she'll make sure we get our share. She'll also be the pathologist responsible for matching marrow donors.'

Now, despite the grudge she felt against Josh for not including her from the start, a new flutter of excitement started in Kirsten's chest. This time it was generated by the prospect of working with these children for whom conventional methods of chemo and radiation had failed. This was not so much a second chance at life: in most cases it was their only chance.

Because patients receiving bone-marrow or stem cell transplants required extensive preliminary treatment before the transplant, then even more careful hospitalisation after it, they were long-term patients, and helping them through their hospitalisation was a change from her usual role of helping patients prepare for their return home. This was the kind of challenge she'd always wanted—the kind of thing she'd dreamed of doing when she'd first decided to study occupational therapy.

Josh was talking, responding to questions, and Kirsten, though part of her mind registered just how deep and assured his voice was, began to consider ways and means of keeping very ill children occupied, entertained and in any way distracted from their aches, pains and illness.

And helping the parents cope with the stress and trauma of it all.

This was what she'd studied—specialised in—now she'd be getting the chance to put some of it into practice.

'Kirsten, could I see you for a moment?'

Once again Josh's voice broke into her thoughts. She looked around and realised people were leaving. She stood up to let Betty get past her, then with a reluctance more physical than mental she edgily approached the desk at the front of the room.

'Did you listen to one word I said?' Josh demanded, those, oh, so blue eyes glaring accusingly at her. 'If you're not interested in this project, just say so right now. First you're furious because I wasn't going to choose you. Now from the bored look on your face when I was describing what we had to do, you couldn't give a damn. Perhaps in spite of that master's degree, you're nothing more than the good-time girl you're reputed to be.'

Kirsten was lost for words at this attack but only momentarily.

'A good-time girl?' she retorted, shocked and infuriated by his glib assassination of her character. 'This from the man who's having an early mid-life crisis, judging by his choice of vehicle? If I *was* thinking of other things, it was of what I can do to make the patients' lives more bearable during their hospitalisation. Now, did you want me for something or did you ask me to wait so you could tell me you didn't fancy the expression on my face, and to insult my reputation?'

She was practically shaking with the fury his words had suddenly unleashed, and though she was aware Josh was trying to speak, she couldn't hear for the rage thundering in her ears.

'You're being irrational,' Josh said coldly.

'*I'm* being irrational? I didn't start this personal stuff. All I want is a place on this team and an opportunity to do some really worthwhile work.'

His smile caught her off guard.

'Me, too,' he said. 'I'm sorry. I've had a lot of late nights, getting the ground rules hammered out for the unit. Every department in the hospital wanted a bit of it, but it needed to be centralised and have all the patients under the one team. Given the fragility of precariously ill and long-term hospitalised children, if we don't all work together—if team splits occur—the whole thing can fail.'

The next smile, an obvious 'please forgive me' ploy, brought the wobbles back to her knees, but she managed to remain upright, even to accept it with a small smile of her own.

'So, did you want something?'

One answer—'You'—slammed into his head so forcefully he knew he should have said no—or perhaps 'Not really'—and let her go. He could do this, he told himself. He could keep her on the team but not get personally involved with her at all.

Or practically not at all.

Especially now she was engaged!

Which was good, he'd decided during the sleepless hours of the previous night, because maybe now he'd stop thinking about her, comparing other women he'd dated to her.

He'd reminded himself of how volatile she was—and how impossible a long-term relationship with someone like that would be for someone like him…

'I do need to talk to you,' he said, when he realised she was standing by the desk, tapping a bright scarlet sandal to indicate impatience—no doubt in case he missed the 'what now' look on her face. 'I've a meeting with

Maintenance, and I'd like your input about the design of the physical space the unit will need. We're taking the western end of ward 6C, and they have to do a certain amount of construction to give us a couple of laminar air-flow rooms for the strictest isolation immediately pre-and post-transplant. Then the rest of the unit will be under a controlled air-flow system with strict protection isolation.'

She didn't answer immediately, which bothered him. Given that the psychosocial well-being of patients came with an OT's charter, and she claimed to have specialised in long-term hospitalisation, why was she thinking about his request?

'Well?' Josh demanded, when the silence, though probably no longer than a couple of seconds, seemed to have stretched for days. 'Do you want the job in the unit, or don't you? And if so, is there something desperately urgent that will prevent you coming to a meeting with the head of Maintenance?'

'Of course I want the job! I thought we settled that yesterday,' she snapped. 'But you spring something like this Maintenance thing on me without giving me time to prepare anything. To think about the mechanics of isolation within the context of the physical space. At what stage would the kids move into the second area—the strict protection isolation? Are they mobile by then? Could we have space for integration with other patients and their parents and possibly siblings, or will that be a restricted area as well? And how long term is long term as far as the isolation goes? You dump this on me without any warning and expect me to be able to talk to Maintenance about it.'

Josh smiled at her indignation and felt the familiar strangeness in his chest as her anger brought a flush to the fine skin on her cheeks and darkened the sprinkling of freckles that spanned her elegant nose.

'Only about the first rooms,' he said, turning his mind firmly away from freckles and the delights of Kirsten's nose, as an echo of his father's warning whispered in his head. 'About positioning of beds, space for a single visitor at a time, perhaps some ideas for making the room interesting to a very sick child who has nothing to do but lie and look at the four walls.'

'Oh, well, that's easy.' Kirsten relented. 'I've been thinking about that stuff for years—did a paper on it last year. I'd like to see puzzles—not like snakes and ladders, but the equipment maybe boxed and painted so looking at it in different ways can produce different pictures and patterns. And maybe something like a hand-held—'

Josh held up his hand.

'Come with me and tell Maintenance.'

Kirsten hesitated. 'Come with me and tell Maintenance' could hardly be classed as the sexiest invitation in the world, so why was her stomach cramping and her skin doing little shivery stuff?

And shouldn't being engaged to Grant have stopped this nonsensical reaction to Josh?

'OK,' she said, then felt immensely better as she saw him frown. Her 'OK' had held the lack of enthusiasm a visit to the dentist usually provoked, and Josh had obviously picked up on it.

They walked through along the corridor to the west wing of the children's wards, and through Ward 6C to the end where a suited man with a roll of plans tucked under his arm waited with a man in overalls. Josh performed the introductions then Bill, the suit, took over, explaining how the small section of the ward would be adapted to rooms with special air flow and air filters to minimise the risks of infection. Screens, curtains, wash-basins for staff and visitors would all have to be designed to make the space as sterile as possible in order to prevent infecting small patients who had no immunity at all.

Bill passed a copy of the plans to Josh, who handed them on to Kirsten.

'If you could get together with Betty and talk about these from the nursing point of view, I'd be grateful. If there are any major changes, get back to me as soon as possible, then perhaps by Friday you'll have furnishing and decorating suggestions as well.'

It was a dismissal, and though she felt contrarily put out, she was also relieved to be getting away from Josh. The darned engagement ring wasn't doing much to help her as far as her reactions to him were concerned.

Betty was at the nurses' station, and Kirsten, aware she had work to do in another department and a lot of tidying up of files and treatment plans, made arrangements to discuss the plans with Betty over lunch.

'Come here if you like,' Betty suggested. 'I can order sandwiches for both of us and our tearoom's nearly always empty at that time. We can spread the plans out on the table and have a good look at them.'

'I'm like a bloody yo-yo!' Kirsten muttered to herself as she headed back up to the OT Department where Clare asked for the student rosters she hadn't finished the previous day, then told her Marion wanted her to see the OT who would be taking on her stroke patients.

'She's down on the ward now,' the secretary told Kirsten, 'so you might go down and fill her in on anything she needs to know, and if you could let us have all the files by tomorrow morning...'

More like Superwoman than a yo-yo, Kirsten decided, but she didn't argue over the files—there were too many other things she didn't know and Clare was the most likely source of information.

'As the rooms aren't built yet, this project won't be getting under way for a while. What am I supposed to do until then?'

Clare shrugged.

'Hang around in Kids, I guess,' she said. 'Make yourself useful down there. Yesterday afternoon, Marion was told that you'd been seconded to the new project as from today, which isn't too good considering we'll need another general-purpose OT to take your place, and the budget's already shot to hell.'

'So why did Marion agree?' Kirsten asked. 'I could have stayed on here at least until the physical work on the ward is completed.'

'It's a big project for the hospital and one that's likely to get heaps of publicity—which is always good for funding purposes. Providing it's good publicity, of course. I think the powers that be are anxious to get it right, so it will be good publicity.'

'Of course, that's far more important than getting it right for the sake of the patients, who just might die if we get it wrong,' Kirsten grumbled, disturbed as ever by the commercialisation of medicine.

'These special projects cost a lot of money—and someone has to pay!' Clare reminded her.

Kirsten nodded and walked away. She had far too much to do to be arguing with the secretary, no matter how she felt about the publicity issue.

Jenny Salter, a young OT who'd joined the team when Kirsten had taken leave the previous year, was talking to Mr Spellman, Kirsten's favourite stroke patient.

'So, you're leaving us,' he said, holding out his left

hand to greet her. His speech was still garbled, but Kirsten had spent enough time with him to understand the words.

'I'm not going far—just to another floor. Back to work with kids. I know I've told you how much I enjoyed that.'

She took his hand and felt his fingers grip hers. She understood what he was feeling and regretted that she had to hand him over to Jenny. Patients became close to their nurses, but stroke patients grew even closer to the various therapists who worked one on one with them, helping them regain the skills they'd need in order to function once they left the hospital.

'I'll still pop up and visit you whenever I can,' she promised, then, as an aide came in and put Mr Spellman's morning tea down on the table, she added, 'Now, let's show Jenny just how well you can handle your cuppa.'

By breaking even the easiest of tasks down into small segments, OTs were able to teach—or re-teach in a lot of cases—the skills their clients would need. Kirsten now watched with pride as Mr Spellman managed, if somewhat shakily, to pick up his specially structured cup and lift it to his lips.

She went around the ward with Jenny, filling her in on the particular problems each patient was having, giving little personal details and comments that wouldn't have been included in the patient files.

By the time she finished she was running late for her meeting with Betty, but she knew the nurse would understand. Not running late would be more surprising in a hospital setting.

CHAPTER THREE

BETTY was in the tearoom, with the plans spread out on the low coffee-table. She was sitting in a comfortable chair at one end, and motioned Kirsten to the two-seater settee.

'Just the day we want it, someone's got a huge pile of files on the big table,' Betty complained, waving her hand to a pile that had slid sideways and was now occupying the entire table and was in danger of invading the floor as well.

'This is probably more comfortable,' Kirsten assured her, taking a sandwich from the proffered plate and nodding affirmatively to coffee when she saw it was in a filter-pot.

She was bent over the plans, chewing on a sandwich and thinking how *she'd* feel cooped up in a sterile room, when the door opened and footsteps crossed towards them.

'Shove over,' a deep voice said, and ripples that were anything but comfortable spread across her skin. She shifted, but as Josh sat down beside her, she realised it wasn't far enough. Mind you, Mexico probably wouldn't have been far enough, but to have him so close his shirt-sleeve brushed against her arm... And his head, as he, too, bent towards the plans to study them, was within kissing distance...

Kirsten straightened, the fingers of her right hand going automatically to the ring on her left, as if touching this talisman might bring her luck. Not that Josh was likely to vanish in a puff of white smoke, but perhaps she'd stop reacting to him if she kept her thoughts on Grant.

No, damn it all! That was wrong! Her thoughts should be on the plans, on the project, on this great new challenge in her working life! She closed her eyes, breathed deeply, then forced herself to focus on the fact that this was the kind of thing she'd always wanted to do. Focus, that's all she needed.

Though it wasn't easy with Josh's body pressed against hers on the settee.

Another deep breath, then she leant forward and tapped the papers.

'I think at this stage, when we're talking physical space, Betty would have more input than me, so why don't we swap places?'

She stood up before Betty could argue, and moved away from the distraction that was Josh. Only problem now, she realised when she settled into Betty's chair, was that she had to look at him.

Josh was pleased Kirsten had moved. It made it easier to concentrate on the plans. When she'd mentioned her psychology studies yesterday, he'd known he'd have to have her on the team—and he'd admitted to himself she'd have been the best person for the job even without the degree. So—finally—he'd put professionalism, and the success of the unit, before his own contradictory feelings about her.

Now 'contradictory' didn't begin to describe his feelings. It was the huge rock she was flashing on her left hand that had thrown him into turmoil, though, from one point of view, an engaged—and therefore off-limits—Kirsten should be easier to work with than the single version.

'So you see,' Betty was saying, pointing to the space

designated for sterile linens on the plans, 'this is imprac-
tical. They should be kept within the positive air pressure
area or you negate the effect of the sterilisation.'

'They could go here,' Kirsten suggested, leaning forward so Josh caught a glimpse of lightly tanned breasts
in the opening of her shirt. 'In this area between the outer
door and the curtain.'

Off-limits, Josh reminded himself, turning one hundred
per cent of his attention to the plans.

They discussed various uses of the space available for
an hour, finally coming up with a list of recommendations
to go to Maintenance.

'Now, let's meet our patients,' Josh suggested, when
Kirsten looked as if she was about to depart. 'Betty, you
know which ones we're considering.'

Betty led the way back to the ward, stopping so they
could all wash their hands before entering even the play
area, where children in various stages of treatment for
cancers ranging from leukaemia to brain tumours either
played together, or lay and watched others playing.

Josh found the little girl he was seeking, a six-year-old
with ALL, acute lymphoblastic leukaemia, due to go
home the following day.

'You might remember Arabella,' he said to Kirsten. 'I
think you were here when she had her first dose of
chemo.'

He watched as Kirsten knelt beside the child.

'Hello, Arabella,' she said. 'Do you still have your
puppy? Cuddles, wasn't that his name?'

Arabella beamed and nodded her head.

'Only he's not a puppy any more—he's grown up.
Come and I'll show you a photo.'

She took Kirsten's hand, leading her towards her bed
and the small cabinet beside it.

'See,' she said, pointing to a photo of a goofy-looking dog, part black Labrador and part poodle. 'There he is.'

The photo must have given Kirsten an idea, for she turned to Josh, excitement glowing in her eyes.

'How's the budget? Do we have the money for frills or should I go begging for some? I've—'

Arabella tugged at her hand, and Kirsten immediately turned her attention back to the small patient, bending to listen as Arabella named all the others in her portrait gallery.

'We'll talk later,' Josh said, as his pager vibrated against his chest. Ten to one it was his secretary reminding him of his two o'clock appointment. 'I'll be in touch.'

Kirsten watched him walk away, but ideas were coming so quickly she hadn't time to feel either relieved or deprived by his departure.

Which in itself was a relief!

Betty took over the introductions, explaining, when Kirsten met four-year-old Jack Webster in an isolation room to one side of the ward, that he'd already had two remissions and as his most recent radiation and chemo treatments had failed, he was first on the list for bone marrow.

'His relatives are all being tested now, and if we don't find a donor from within them, we'll go to the donor bank. He's the reason Josh is rushing this unit into existence. He might seem laid back about it, but he'll hound those maintenance people until it's all fitted out and ready for use. He's hoping to be ready to start pre-transplant treatment as soon as possible.'

Kirsten knew Betty was talking about preparations for the child's body to receive the donated bone marrow. These preparations were aimed at eliminating or at least minimising post-transplant complications. As all the existing bone marrow in the child's body would have to be destroyed in order to kill all cancerous cells, Jack would have no immunity and would be prey to any infection he might pick up.

She sighed as she looked at the sleeping child, and saw Mrs Webster nod.

' I sigh a lot as well,' the other woman said. 'And wish it could be me, not him. But not a lot of wishes come true, do they?'

'What does Jack like?' Kirsten asked, staying on with the woman though Betty excused herself to answer a nurse's query.

'Anything with wheels—the bigger the better,' Mrs Webster replied. 'Big diggers, the kind of trucks with wheels like houses, that they use in the mines. All his favourite picture books have mechanical things in them.'

Kirsten felt her excitement levels rise. The more she thought about it, the more she could visualise the rooms where these children would be isolated before, during and after their treatment.

So by the time she was ready to leave the hospital, two hours after her usual time of six o'clock, the excitement was still simmering in her body, and the extra work of preparing her patient files to be passed over to Jenny hadn't tired her as much as she'd expected.

'I tried to phone you but you weren't answering your extension.'

Josh's voice sent her spinning—around to see him and inwardly as well. Maybe she was more tired than she thought.

She eyed him warily.

'You had some ideas—wondered about money. Are you on your way somewhere?'

'Home for dinner before I starve to death,' Kirsten told

him, pleased that after the initial shock of having him creep up behind her she was functioning quite well.

'Is your significant other waiting for you there?' Josh shot a cool glance towards her left hand. 'Or could I buy you dinner? Perhaps at that place on the ground floor of your building—Mickey's? Purely business—to discuss your ideas.'

Was it her imagination, or had Josh sounded a little put out when he'd mentioned her 'significant other'?

And was it OK for an engaged woman to have dinner with another man?

Particularly when the other man in question was one she'd lusted over for the past year?

She couldn't believe all the matters like this that had never come up in any of the quizzes she'd ever done—'Are you committed to your relationship?'—or in her mother's books on etiquette, which she'd dutifully studied while still at school.

Though neither the quizzes nor the books had ever mentioned lust as a contributing factor or a deterrent to either successful relationships or proper engagement behaviour. While none of her psychology studies had ever provided a logical explanation for the phenomenon.

'Well?'

The demand, recalling a similar one a lot earlier in this exciting day, broke into thoughts which, while not currently lustful, weren't far off.

'I guess we could talk about it over dinner,' she agreed, then was surprised when he laughed.

'Hey, don't overwhelm me with enthusiasm here. It might go straight to my head.'

He took her arm and held it as they crossed the road, and the physical contact put all Kirsten's senses on alert.

'As if you need my enthusiasm to get a swollen head!

You're adored by all the nursing staff, pandered to by all the junior medical staff and have women falling over themselves to ride beside you in that black beast you call a car.'

'That's the second dig today about my car. Did you hate it—back when we went out? Why didn't you say so? I could have driven it with the top up, you know. Then it's just like an ordinary sedan.'

'Very ordinary,' Kirsten said dryly. 'And speaking of cars, where is the chariot tonight? We seem to be walking towards my building, rather than driving. I didn't know you could walk.'

'Not fair. I always do the hospital fund-raising walka-thon, and the car's up in the car park, but when I saw you heading out of the building I wanted to catch up, and by the time I'd fetched it you'd have gone.'

This is totally weird, Kirsten decided. Here I am, walk-ing home with Josh, about to have dinner with him, which is like all my fantasies coming true, and, yes, I'm twitchy, but I'm not delirious with excitement.

She rubbed her thumb across the inside of her engage-ment ring and smiled to herself. Maybe it *was* working. Maybe being engaged to Grant would finally lay the spectre of her attraction to Josh—now and for ever. Though Josh had been the last person on her mind when Grant had sprung his surprise on her.

Lost in thought, and only half tuned in to Josh's con-versation—something to do with Arabella and a new baby in the family, its umbilical cord blood frozen for use as a transplant if this second remission didn't last—Kirsten was making the obligatory noises required to keep the conversation going, and conjuring up Grant's features in her head.

So Josh's sharp 'Look out!' then the fiercely muttered

'Bloody idiot!' took a while to register, by which time, in spite of Josh pulling her to one side, the long, lean youth on the skateboard had hurtled into her, sending her flying towards the gutter and the traffic on the busy road.

'Don't try to get up, just sit a minute.'

Josh squatted beside her, his arm around her shoulders, his free hand smoothing back her hair. She was sitting on the kerb but had little recollection of how she'd got there, though mud streaks on one of her favourite skirts suggested she'd been in the gutter at some stage.

'Are you hurt or just shaken?' Josh asked, his eyes, even in the shadowy light, dark with worry.

Cautiously, Kirsten moved her limbs and found everything functioning.

'I think I'm OK, but I'd prefer to be standing,' she replied, conscious of people gathering to look at her.

Josh helped her to her feet, and the onlookers, satisfied there'd be no further show once she'd taken a couple of steps towards the safety of the other side of the footpath, moved away. He led her up the steps into the apartment building—she hadn't realised they were so close to home—but when he opened the door leading into Mickey's bar and bistro she shook her head.

'No. I need to clean up first.'

He understood and summoned the lift, still holding her elbow, but before it arrived, and straight after she'd assured Josh, for the twentieth time, that she was all right, the trembling started, bones and muscles all shaking so uncontrollably she was grateful when he put his arms around her and held her close.

His body pressed against hers, providing the support she needed, feeding assurance until the shakes began to lessen.

'This is stupid. I'll be OK, truly I will. And the lift's here. I need to get out of this foyer.'

The words, muffled by suit material as her face pressed against his shoulder, were barely audible, but he must have heard, for he stroked her back and murmured, 'Hush. We'll go soon. When you're ready.'

He was brushing little kisses—soothing kisses—on her hair, and his voice was so husky she knew he, too, had had a shock. But worst of all was the realisation that she was no longer pressed hard against Josh's body because without it she wouldn't be able to stay upright—but rather because it was where she wanted to be, and, now it had stopped shaking, her body was enjoying it enormously, thank you very much.

A word she rarely used echoed fiercely in her head.

You're an engaged woman, the head voice scolded. You don't need quizzes or etiquette books to tell you this is wrong. Get your act together here!

Feebly, because her body's opinion was so at odds with her mind's, she pushed away.

'I'm OK now—fine. But maybe we could talk about those ideas some other time.'

Josh stepped away from her at the first sign of resistance, making her realise he'd only been providing support—while somehow holding the lift doors open? Maybe with his foot?

'Of course,' he agreed, leading her into the cubicle, pressing the requisite buttons, then ushering her out into the small fourth-floor foyer, 'but I'm not leaving you like this. I'll come in with you while you shower and get comfortable, then I'll order our dinners and bring them up to your flat. That way I get to eat as well as keeping an eye on you for an hour or so—in case of a delayed reaction. You did hit your head as you fell.'

Kirsten combed her fingers through her hair, feeling for any sign that this might be true. There was a sore spot and a small bump developing—but bad enough for Josh to stay?

She knew she should argue, assure him she was fine, but remembering how good it had been to be held in his arms made her hesitate and the moment for saying no was lost. Besides, he'd taken her bunch of keys out of her still unsteady fingers and was trying each in turn in the lock.

And making so much noise it was only a matter of time before someone in the flat opposite came out to see what was happening.

And who was that someone likely to be?

Only Gabi, sister of the man to whom Kirsten was engaged, and confidante from the time when Kirsten had wept buckets of tears over this same Josh Phillips!

Kirsten's stomach twisted. If she'd been able to render Josh invisible, she would have, because no matter how innocent all this was, she was ninety-nine per cent sure it wouldn't look that way to Gabi.

'You're not all right!' Josh said crossly, and Kirsten realised she was standing like a grubby statue outside her door, which Josh had finally opened and now held patiently. When she failed to move, he took over, grasping her elbow again, ushering her into the flat, murmuring encouragement.

Josh's fussing was nice, even if he didn't know the cause of the acceleration of her wreckage. But now, though saved from discovery in the foyer, she had to worry about Gabi visiting later—perhaps while she and Josh were sharing a cosy meal. Or Gabi meeting Josh when he was coming back up in the lift with dinner for two. How would that look to a fiancé's sister?

Summoning all her scattered wits and reserves of energy, she straightened up, stepped away from Josh then turned to face him.

'I'm OK now, really I am. Why don't you go down and have a drink at Mickey's and I'll have a quick shower, change and join you in—say, fifteen minutes? I do want to talk about the unit and some of the things I'd like to suggest might have to be incorporated into the design of the rooms, so the sooner we discuss it the better.'

She all but pushed him out the door, which prompted Josh to wonder if she was expecting the man who'd paid big bucks for that ring to appear at any moment. But if that happened, how would she explain her sudden departure to meet him for dinner downstairs?

He puzzled over it as he made his way back to the bistro, then decided to put it down to typical irrational female behaviour. In fact, it was good they were eating downstairs for whatever reason, because as he'd held her in his arms earlier he'd somehow forgotten not only that she was engaged but that he couldn't afford to be distracted by whatever magnetism drew him to her. And though he'd been... What had he been? Frustrated certainly. Aggravated—yes, that, too—and infinitely put out by her refusal to have a brief affair with him, he'd come to be thankful to her. Sensible reasoning, and a good dollop of hindsight, had convinced him that Kirsten Collins was definitely off-limits to a man who'd made a rational decision not to marry—or at least to put off marriage until he was forty.

Until then he'd enjoy the company of women who understood the rules of short relationships, which wasn't hard, as his reputation as a man who shunned commitment preceded him wherever he went.

He was happy enough to live with that reputation, though it made more of his exploits than he'd actually enjoyed, and the relationships were usually ended by the women in question when they realised how much his working life interfered with socialising! But the question of marriage was different. His own childhood experience had proved how hard it was for a man to be a successful specialist *and* a father to a young family at the same time. He knew other people did it—and other specialists seemed to cope—but his family was genetically challenged when it came to doing two things well at once. Hopeless, in fact.

His grandfather had started the tradition, stowing his wife and children on a property outside town but living in town himself and visiting at weekends. So Josh's own father had seen nothing wrong in acting the same way, though *his* duty visits, as his sons had grown older, had become less and less frequent until his parents would have to have been considered separated.

Was it because he was the youngest child that he'd picked up on his mother's unhappiness? And why, when it hadn't seemed to bother his older brothers, had *he* missed having a real father, someone there more of the time, someone who showed love in other ways than occasional visits to the hospital, where the Phillips heritage was pointed out? A father whose sole contribution to Josh's struggle through adolescence had been 'Don't mess with redheads'?

From an early age Josh had known he was expected to follow his forebears and brothers into medicine. But he'd also figured out that his children, if he had them, would have a very different kind of father.

The way he planned it, by the time he was forty he'd have achieved what he wanted to in his career, kept faith with tradition, and he could go into teaching and cut back on patient time. Then, maybe, he'd consider having children because then he'd be able to give them the kind of love and attention he'd found so lacking in his own childhood.

And with his children thus relegated to the future, he reinstated his image of the 'perfect wife'—a calm, controlled, quiet, intelligent and undemanding woman—blonde, or maybe brunette—back into his head. She would fit into his life as unobtrusively as well-made furniture, caring for the children, entertaining his colleagues, running his home with the smooth, unruffled efficiency he liked in his life.

It was laughable to imagine the bright but erratic star that was Kirsten in such a role—impossible!

Having sorted all that out—again—Josh walked into Mickey's in a buoyant mood, secure in the knowledge that common sense had won out again.

Though common sense had a battle remembering all the plus factors in this theory when Kirsten joined him. She'd showered and her hair was wet around the edges, so strands of it clung damply to her skin around the hairline, framing her face and making her seem so much younger than her twenty-eight years. And lack of makeup gave her an air of innocence that caused strange spasms in his gut—or maybe that was hunger.

Whatever it was, it was preferable to the definitely sexual stirrings in another part of his anatomy—responding, as it had in the lift, to the lush, shapely body, decently covered yet somehow revealed by a dress that skimmed over it like a second skin, clinging to the fullness of her breasts, the rounded arc of her hips, ending far too soon so legs as long as tomorrow couldn't help but claim his attention.

'Do you want a drink?' he asked, gulping down the last

of the light beer he'd ordered and wishing it was something stronger.

She shook her head, the dry bits of the red-brown hair swinging out a little with the movement, then she greeted Mickey with a smile and asked what specials he had on offer, displaying no more interest in Josh the man than she had in the barstool she'd settled on.

'Arabella's photos gave me the idea,' she said, firing more disappointment in Josh's chest as she launched straight into business once they'd both ordered meals.

'The kids love having photos and cards and pictures, but in the most sterile of rooms they're not allowed. You have the walls and ceiling which can be painted, but paintings are static. What if we had a video machine, the kind they have in discos, showing the latest music videos up on a wall? The rooms already have a control unit with the bed and call button controls. We could scan pictures of the patient's family, or his or her favourite books, into the machine and with different channels to choose from, the machine could direct personal photos or pictures into each room.'

'Could they move the pictures—throw them onto the ceiling as well as the wall?' He was hooked. Her idea might prove expensive but it was definitely better thinking about money than remembering how much he'd longed to get Kirsten into his bed. And wondering what it would have been like if...

'Are you listening?' she demanded, then she shrugged her shoulders and rolled her eyes. 'Honestly! Men! You ask a question then go off into another world instead of listening to the answer. Do you want to know more about it or don't you?'

Embarrassed that his mind had strayed so far so quickly, Josh straightened on the stool, shoved the memories back into the attic of his mind and tried valiantly to remember the question he must have asked.

'Can you move the pictures? That's what you asked, and as I've already explained once, I don't see why not. I think they could also manipulate the images, maybe change the colours or enlarge particular sections. Because it's all computerised, they should be able to do anything that you can do on a computer, and if the images were controlled by touching a sensor pad then the lightest of movements from even the weakest of little fingers could manipulate them.'

He was more than hooked now because he could feel the first glimmers of excitement—work-related this time. Depression was a big problem with very ill children, and when sick and isolated they could lose the will to live that had brought them through the initial stages of their disease.

'Do you want to move to a table?' Mickey asked, gesturing to the other side of the bar where small tables overlooked the building's pool and garden area. 'Your meals are ready.'

Kirsten slid off her stool and moved around the bar, the sway of her body reminding Josh yet again of what they'd almost shared.

Was it because it was an almost, not a done deed, that he was still so attracted to her?

Well, it was too late. That ring she was flaunting held a serious stone, and he guessed she wouldn't have committed herself lightly.

Kirsten approached their table with a dark cloud of disaffection settling around her shoulders. Josh's enthusiasm for her ideas had been underwhelming at best. In fact, he'd drifted off to some other place halfway through the conversation, then had stared at her as if trying to work out who she was for the rest of it.

And even though she was eating with him for purely business reasons, and in a public place, she was still suffering niggling jabs of guilt. Probably because, try as she might to escape or dampen or otherwise diminish it, her body still lusted after the wretched man.

Maybe if they'd gone one week past the month before he'd told her about his anti-commitment stance—if they'd actually had sex—she'd have got it out of her system.

Studying him across the table as he thanked Mickey for their meals, she felt a shiver of anticipation rush down her spine, the result of a stray and quickly quashed thought that maybe that was the answer. Sleep with the man and get him out of her system.

No! her head yelled practically before the thought had formed into words.

'Is there something wrong with it?' Josh asked, and she came back to the present to realise she was toying with her pasta, twisting her fork through the strands of linguini but not lifting any of it to her mouth.

'No, it's fine,' she said, and far too hurriedly forked some into her mouth. So, of course, it dripped everywhere and strands dangled dangerously downwards, no doubt making her look like a drooling idiot.

'Tricky stuff,' Josh teased, and the gentle smile he gave her sent her heart into panic and her pulses racing.

She couldn't be feeling like this about another man when she was engaged to Grant! But as she listened to Josh extolling the deliciousness of his meal, her heart continued to ignore orders to behave, while her fingers showed an alarming desire to creep across the table and rest, for just a moment, on his arm. Right there, on the bit of tanned and slightly hairy skin revealed below the cuff of his white shirt...

Blot both the thought and the image from your mind!

Concentrating on the meal helped, and the pasta was behaving so badly she needed to concentrate.

'I never order stuff in strands for just that reason,' Josh remarked, battling a smile as a tangled forkful of pasta slid traitorously back into her bowl.

'I can usually manage it quite well,' Kirsten told him, though it was better to be making a fool of herself eating uncooperative linguini than running her forefinger over tanned wrist-skin.

Infinitely better than throwing herself into his arms and demanding he take her to bed so she could get him out of her system and get on with loving Grant. 'And aren't we supposed to be discussing the new unit, rather than my lack of finesse with pasta?'

'You've more ideas?' he said, and she frowned at him.

'You don't have to sound so surprised. Even good-time girls—I think that was what you called me—can hold a couple of thoughts together at one time.'

Though with difficulty at the moment!

She concentrated harder.

'My original idea, before I saw Arabella's pictures and considered scanning personal items into a computerised video, was that with the same kind of control a child might be able to alter a light source so it changed the configuration of the room. I'd have to work it out on my computer, but say we painted the walls in geometric patterns, using different colours, then with a simple manipulation of light he or she might be able to make animals or objects appear.'

'I know what you mean, but it sounds complicated.'

Kirsten shrugged.

'So, the older kids could do it, and it would be challenging for them, and with the younger ones, perhaps a visitor could change the lights and leave different pictures showing at different times of the day.'

'I've a cousin who's a computer whiz. I'll put it all to him and see what he has to say. He'd also know what equipment would be needed and how complex it will be.'

Josh smiled at her as if the conversation had been satisfactorily concluded—at least for the moment. Aware of the dangers of silence settling between them, Kirsten picked out the olives and sun-dried tomatoes from her linguini while searching her mind for a new topic to keep thoughts of more personal matters at bay.

'So, when do you expect to be able to start? And do you want me to do pre-procedure stuff with the kids? Most of them are used to all the needles, drips and other paraphernalia of hospitals, so is there anything different you'll be doing?'

Josh studied her for a moment, as if wondering why she was asking, then he lifted one shoulder in a half-shrug and said, 'I thought we might have ended the evening with a bit of light social banter—maybe sharing the latest hospital gossip and scandal.'

'I've been away for a fortnight so I don't know any gossip and scandal. Besides, we're only eating together to discuss the new unit.'

Again he paused before answering, and she could almost feel the blue eyes touching her skin as his gaze swept across her face.

'Yes, I guess we are,' he said softly. 'It's not as if we've anything else in common.'

His voice was low and husky, and it was its timbre as much as the words themselves which made her heart shiver in her chest.

CHAPTER FOUR

BUT when Josh spoke again, he was all business.

'We touched on this at lunch yesterday when I talked about counselling. I'd like you to be an informal liaison person with the parents. You'll be on the ward, doing recreational activities with the other children, or with our special cases before pre-treatment starts, so the parents will be able to talk to you, ask questions, in a less formal way than in the talks I have with them about the actual procedure. It's not counselling as such, but it could be a way of helping the families come to terms with what's happening, and maybe a way for us to gauge how the parents are thinking and feeling about it.'

Kirsten understood what he meant. Most parents tended to see the nursing and medical staff as very busy people, so avoided questioning them too often, and while they could make an appointment to see a counsellor, the meeting would take them off the ward—away from their child. But the OT was seen as someone there merely to play with the kids, and she could direct play and talk at the same time.

'I'm happy to do that,' she said, pushing her plate away as the linguini finally defeated her. 'But I'd better do some reading up on what's involved so I don't give them the wrong information.'

Josh nodded.

'I'll give you some books and then, some time this week, run through it all with you. You understand the concept?'

Kirsten heard the excitement in his voice—for someone who avoided commitment in his private life, he had it by the truckload where work was concerned.

'It's based on the fact that the poisonous effects of chemo and radiation limit its uses, but if we have donor material we can do full-body radiation and or toxic levels of chemo, destroying all bone marrow and cancerous cells but in the process destroying all the things that keep us alive. Then by infusing bone marrow into the blood, we start new marrow regenerating in the child's body and, hopefully, provide a chance of a full recovery.'

Josh nodded.

'A lot of people don't understand the severity of what we're doing. They know more about, so think in terms of, organ transplants, but organ transplants are easy compared to this. I mean, a donated kidney, once properly attached within a recipient's body, will begin to work almost immediately, but bone marrow isn't like that. It's not even transplanted in the true sense of the word. We infuse it into the blood, then the stem cells, which are the useful part of it, make their way slowly to the host's bone, then, even more slowly, have to regenerate before they become useful.'

'That's if they don't reject the host body—it's the opposite to what happens with other transplants, isn't it?' Kirsten said, having read up on it when little Nathan had been so ill. 'The new material rejects the old.'

'They call it GVHD, graft versus host disease. And that's just one of the problems,' Josh agreed, but far from sounding defeated, he made it sound as if it was a war he had to wage—and that he was armed and ready for it.

His tone re-ignited Kirsten's own excitement. The opportunity to be part of this was bigger than the silly feelings she'd had for Josh, and with Grant so far away, and only in the city for occasional visits, she'd have the time and energy to devote herself entirely to the project—to really throw herself into work.

'So, you see,' she said to Gabi later, when, needing to talk to someone about it, she'd popped, after knocking properly, into her friend's flat, 'it all fits in so well, and it's the kind of thing I've always wanted to do. The kids need to be isolated for some seven to ten days before the transplant, then three to five weeks afterwards, so they need a lot of supportive therapy. As well as the images on the walls, if I can swing that, I'll need other ideas for keeping their minds off their poor sick bodies.'

'It sounds fantastic from the challenge side of it, but these kids are very ill and some of them won't make it. Are you prepared for that?'

Kirsten nodded.

'I know I was upset before, when kids I'd worked with died, but with these particular patients it's different because without the transplant they've no chance at all.'

Gabi smiled and gave her a hug, then stepped away.

'And Grant—where does he fit into this grand new life? Did you two make any plans?'

Kirsten rubbed her thumb across the inside of the gold band of her engagement ring.

'Plans? Please! I didn't know we were engaged until he was getting into his plane. We've actually got to get to know each other a bit better before we talk about marriage. But before the ring was produced, when we were just interested in each other, he said he'd be down in a couple of months, then for the agricultural show in August.'

She grinned at Gabi.

'In between, I guess we're stuck with phone sex.'

She laughed at the shocked expression on her friend's

face. 'Of course we don't—well, not yet, anyway. Most
of the time when he phones, it's to tell me how his day
has been. He comes in at dusk, has a shower, then sits on
the veranda with a drink and rings me up—says it relaxes
him after a busy day— Oh!'

'What's up?' Gabi asked, but Kirsten was too busy remembering—and wondering what to do next—to answer.

When Grant had phoned the previous evening, she'd
insisted it was her turn next, and had promised to phone
him at seven-thirty. As it was now after ten…

'What time do farmers go to bed?' she asked Gabi, her
voice so weak with guilt it was a wonder her friend heard
it.

'Earlier than this—but don't worry. You can talk tomorrow night. Or email him. He'll understand work had
to come first. Wait till the cattle muster starts. You'll be
lucky if you hear from him for a month.'

Kirsten left, but as Gabi shut the door behind her she
wondered about the long-distance relationship between
her brother and her friend. She'd heard the passion in
Kirsten's voice when she'd talked about the new hospital
project. Kirsten threw herself so wholeheartedly into
everything she did, but would helping Grant on the family
property—eventually—provide her with the same kind of
satisfaction as the work she'd trained for?

If only Alex were here, not on duty, she could talk it
over with him. But she wouldn't mention her other worry
to Alex—the one about Kirsten working so closely with
Josh Phillips.

Again!

Kirsten heard the phone ringing as she unlocked the door,
and raced to answer it. It wasn't Grant, but Josh, to say
he'd spoken to his computer-whiz cousin who felt all the

ideas she'd suggested should be possible, and that he'd be happy to come up with a program.

'The bad news is the cost,' he added, when Kirsten finished expressing her excitement. 'Not for the program, as Matt will do that for us, but the type of machine we'd need to run the programs, allowing different rooms to have different programs showing, would cost about thirty thousand dollars. It's too much to take from the money we've been granted, Kirsten.'

She heard the regret in his voice, and knew he was as disappointed for her as he was for the children they'd be treating.

'Leave that to me,' she told him. 'May I contact your cousin so I can get details of what we need, and which firms manufacture or distribute these machines? Maybe I can wangle a donation, or get some service clubs interested in fund-raising for it.'

They talked on, sparking ideas off each other, discussing strategies for helping parents as well as children cope with the long, drawn-out process of marrow regeneration.

'I'll see you tomorrow, then,' Josh said, when Kirsten, realising an hour had passed and she still had to email Grant, brought the conversation to an end.

The flicker of excitement was purely because of the work—the challenge—she told herself, then, just in case it wasn't, she spent another hour writing a long email to Grant, telling him all about the new job and her ideas for keeping the children occupied during their extended hospitalisation.

That'd serve him right for telling her about the crutching.

Josh finished the email he was sending to a colleague in the US, sent it winging through the ether and pushed his chair back from the desk. He'd wanted to check on some recent research into separating stem cells from the rest of bone marrow, but he knew that if he started, one site would lead to another and he'd be up for half the night.

But if he went to bed, would he sleep? Or would he think of Kirsten, and how she'd felt when he'd held her in his arms?

Trembling in his arms…

He opened a search engine and set it to tracking down the latest information. Better to put his sleeplessness to some use.

Betty was on duty in Ward 6C when Kirsten arrived for duty next morning.

'Josh left a heap of books and papers for you. They're in the tearoom. He said it's a good thing you like learning because there's heaps there, and he's marked the interesting bits.'

Kirsten nodded, relieved to hear Josh had already visited the ward. She'd brought her laptop to work, intending to have a fiddle with some designs for the walls, but now, if she had any spare time, she'd be reading up on bone-marrow transplants instead.

As part of her 'being available' to parents, she was taking over all the OT work in 6C, so she began her 'real' work with a quick read-through of the notes left by the previous incumbent. She was pleased to see the play therapy program she'd devised more than twelve months ago was still being followed, though naturally adapted to meet the needs of whoever was in the ward at the time.

A number of children on the ward had been diagnosed early in their lives with some form of cancer. Hospitalisation and treatment had interrupted the stages of their physical development, and some of them were behind in both their fine motor skills, which controlled things like finger movement, and their gross motor skills—walking, running, climbing. Because practising these skills helped with the development of a child's brain, it was important to interest them in games that incorporated different movements.

As Kirsten read through the notes, she got a better idea of the children with whom she'd be working, and their developmental stages. The older ones required very little OT as such, though strategies for oral care were important, and care of the shunt, a small plastic tube inserted for ease of delivering drugs, which a number of them had implanted in their chests, was also essential.

Teenagers, eager to be like their peers, could sometimes neglect these things. Just as those on oral medication—usually for acute lymphoblastic leukaemia, which required up to two years of daily tablet-taking—often neglected to take their tablets. As many as one in five behaved this way, according to one survey done in the UK.

For a few minutes she puzzled over how this could be overcome—could she persuade those in the danger ages to treat the tablets as vitamins and take them automatically? Or devise some interesting form of reminder like a watch alarm, so, instead of seeing themselves as 'different', they could see themselves as 'special'.

Or a peer partner who oversaw the taking of medication? Would that be more acceptable to a teenager?

Realising it wasn't a problem that could be solved immediately, she set it aside for the moment, hoping her subconscious might come up with something, and again read through the patient notes.

Having only one new patient in the ward made Kirsten's choice of who to see first easy.

'The chemotherapy not only destroys cancerous cells,

it destroys a lot of good cells as well,' she explained a
little later to Lily, a thirteen-year-old admitted for her first
treatment for the second most common childhood cancer,
acute myeloid leukaemia, or AML. The young girl was
pale and tired-looking, and had been sitting up in bed as
if not sure what else there was to do.

'And because it affects the mucous lining in your
mouth, it can cause mouth ulcers and other irritations—
very painful stuff! That's why looking after your mouth
is very important.'

She took Lily through the procedure, showing her sam-
ples of the mouthwash, antifungal gel and lozenges that
patients used. Lily asked questions, mostly about her treatment, but of course the subject of hair loss, always a major
concern for a teenager, came up.

'It looks to me as if you've got a great-shaped head,'
Kirsten told her, feeling Lily's head so the girl didn't think
it a patronising conversational gambit. 'And shaved heads,
both for males and females, are far more common now.
It doesn't automatically label you as a cancer sufferer.'

'I know—I'm looking forward to it,' Lily said. 'I
wanted to shave my head last year for the cancer appeal,
but Mum wouldn't let me so I cut it really short and dyed
it green. But once I'm bald I'm going to get a tattoo right
here.'

She pointed to a spot behind her left ear.

'Try a stick-on one first,' Kirsten suggested. 'I know
there's less emphasis on steering clear of infection these
days, but getting a real tattoo with a real tattoo needle and
real ink might be pushing the envelope a little. I'm sure
Dr Phillips wouldn't approve.'

'You mean Josh? He told me to call him Josh. Isn't
he dishy? Wouldn't you kill to end up with a fellow
like him?'

'Perhaps not kill,' Kirsten said faintly. 'And wait until you meet Dr Granger—he's the resident attached to this ward. Tall and dark with those smouldering kind of eyes.'

'Talking about me, are you, girls?'

As Kirsten spun to confront the first man they'd been discussing, she wondered how much he'd heard.

'Your eyes don't smoulder,' she told him firmly, hoping to counter the look of adoration Lily was giving him.

'I bet I could make them smoulder,' he said, turning to Lily and pulling such an appalling face she giggled helplessly.

Lily's mother arrived at that moment, and though she waited to be introduced, as soon as the civilities were done, Kirsten excused herself and moved away. Children not scheduled for treatment were gathering in the play area in the centre of the ward, while others were already hooked up to bags of fluid, enduring the slow drip of the chemical cocktails into their blood.

Arabella, so slight it was a wonder her bones didn't break, was organising the others, setting up a 'school'. Kirsten took her place as a pupil, and from her small chair guided and encouraged the children to use various muscle groups in their play.

Parents came in, those whose children were long-term patients less obviously stressed now they knew the system. They settled by their child's bed if he or she was receiving treatment or too ill from the after-effects to participate in the games. Others joined Kirsten as 'pupils' at Arabella's school, delighting the little girl by entering into the spirit of the game.

By lunchtime Kirsten was feeling the effects of the physical exercise. She'd led the children, an aide and a couple of parents on a 'follow the leader' through and around the various bits of equipment in the ward.

'Strokes was never this energetic,' she said to Betty, who chuckled, though sympathetically.

Sitting down in the tearoom, she checked the pile of books Josh had left. She'd need all her remaining energy just to carry them home. But rather than start on them now, she phoned Josh's cousin to ask who would be most likely to help by providing the equipment they'd need, searched a *Yellow Pages* for the requisite phone numbers, then began to beg.

Experience told her the direct approach was best, so she contacted six firms, asking for the name of the person in charge, and when it might be possible to make an appointment to see him or her. She also explained what she wanted, because busy executives who were giving up their time to see her would need to know why. Going in cold, she'd found, often resulted in a flat and non-negotiable refusal.

In the end, she had four appointments for the following week, and from various junior people knew exactly what she'd need to tell Maintenance in anticipation of getting the equipment.

The afternoon play session was less lively, most of the children content to do puzzles or play games on various hand-held toys. Kirsten sat with Arabella at one of the computers, showing her how to move the mouse and click on it to change the pictures on the screen.

'We have times when the computer has to be pre-booked so all who want a turn get one, and other times when no one's using it.' Sally, a young aide on the ward, came to stand behind them. 'This is the first time Arabella's tried to do things herself.'

Kirsten understood why. Although the mouse was ergonomically correct, it was made that way for an adult hand, and Arabella's small hand, further weakened by her illness, found it difficult to manipulate. When Kirsten had been in the ward previously, she'd had a range of mice available, but rummaging through drawers at the computer desk failed to produce any of them.

She fetched her own laptop, which used a touch sensitive pad to manipulate the cursor, and soon had Arabella shifting images about the screen and opening boxes to reveal new pictures and games.

'The touch pad is obviously the way to go.' This time it was a deeper voice speaking over her shoulder, and the diamond flashing on her finger wasn't enough to stop her skin reacting to his presence, or tiny goose-bumps rising on her forearms.

'Yes,' she said. 'I'm meeting your cousin after work so we'll talk to him about how we can incorporate it into the system.'

'My cousin Matt?'

Josh sounded so surprised Kirsten turned to look at him.

'Yes. We're meeting at Mickey's for a drink and a chat. You gave me his phone number, remember. I've appointments to see some video people next week so I need to know exactly what I'm asking for, and I also want to talk to him about patterns and designs for the wall. I can visualise something like a kaleidoscope but don't know how to go about making that work.'

The explanation didn't help Josh in the slightest. His mind had stalled back when Kirsten had mentioned meeting Matt. It had nothing to do with the fact that Matt had more than his share of the Phillips good looks—he'd probably got a bit of Josh's as well—but he was also the renowned playboy of the clan.

In fact, his reputation was far worse than Josh's own. Single, married or engaged, as far as women were concerned, it made no difference to Matt. Once he saw a woman he fancied, he pursued her with a relentless single-minded intensity which even the most assured and blasé of women seemed to find irresistible.

And it was useless to hope Kirsten wouldn't take his fancy. She was only the most fanciable woman in the entire hospital, red-haired or not!

He hid a groan that threatened to escape, then realised all was not lost. After all, who was the head of this unit? Who would have to approve any expenditure? Even approve the introduction of equipment not essential to the patients' physical health?

He excused himself and left to phone Matt.

Which was his first mistake.

Actually joining them for a drink was the second, he realised much later as he sat and watched his cousin, not at all put out by Josh's presence, flirting with Kirsten.

And Kirsten, engagement ring or not, was flirting right back.

Oh, they might both be pretending they were discussing computer graphics, but he could read the subtext to their conversation about bytes and sites and windows, and he didn't like it. Not one bit.

So when Gabi and Alex Graham walked in, no doubt intending to enjoy a quiet dinner on their own, Josh insisted the Grahams join them for a drink, then suggested perhaps they could all eat together.

'Say yes,' Kirsten whispered under her breath to Gabi, who turned startled brown eyes in her direction.

Kirsten nodded to emphasise the order, and was relieved when Gabi made all the right noises, doing so well anyone not in the know would have thought she was genuinely delighted to have a quiet evening with her husband interrupted.

'Not like you to need rescuing from two handsome

men,' she murmured to Kirsten when the two of them made their excuses and were heading for the cloakroom.

'Oh, give me strength!' Kirsten muttered. 'Here I am, engaged to Grant, out with Matt to find out all kinds of things I really need to know, and he's coming on to me like there's no tomorrow, while Josh, who's turned up totally uninvited, is sitting there glowering at me and all but growling every time Matt opens his mouth.'

She looked despairingly at Gabi.

'I want to know about computer programs and videos and scanners, but the man is making it all sound like an X-rated film script.'

'So, do you want me to ask about scanners and computer programs for you? Steer him back when he goes astray?'

Kirsten hugged her friend.

'If you would, and also, if you wouldn't mind, and I know I shouldn't ask especially when you and Alex are just married again, but could I, please, sit between you? He keeps touching me.'

'Josh keeps touching you?' Gabi made it sound as if such a thing defied belief, but though Kirsten felt an urge to argue that it wasn't so totally unlikely, she knew it was wiser to simply put the matter straight.

'Not Josh, Matt. He's a toucher, so you'd better avoid him as well. What if you sit between Josh and me—Alex, me, you, Josh—that way he can only stroke Josh or Alex's thigh.'

'I don't know about Josh, but Alex would be likely to hit him—or perhaps just say something very rude. Has he really been that bad?'

Gabi sounded so anxious Kirsten had to think before she answered.

'I guess not,' she admitted, 'but I don't want him touching me, which exaggerates things, and there's Josh sitting there with the kind of facial expression people usually reserve for bad fish, making it all so much worse.'

They went back to the table where the conversation had turned to the development of medical equipment based on television and video inventions. But try as Gabi might to juggle the seating, when they moved to their table overlooking the pool Kirsten found herself not between Alex and Gabi, but between Alex and Josh.

'Disappointed you're not next to Matt?' Josh murmured in an undertone only she could hear.

'No!' she murmured back, though for a murmur it managed to hold a fair degree of venom.

'Oh, I thought from what was going on, you and Gabi were trying to arrange it, but in the interests of your fiancé, I felt I should intervene. My cousin Matt—'

'Did I hear my name?'

Matt smiled charmingly across the table. He was certainly good-looking—better-looking, in fact, than Josh—but nothing sparked in her blood when she looked at him.

Josh smiled back.

'I was telling Kirsten that you're no respecter of other men's women, and a little thing like an engagement ring won't keep her safe from your often unwanted attentions.'

'Unwanted attentions?' Matt did shocked very well. 'Utter slander! As if I would! Kirsten and I have been discussing ways and means of entertaining your patients. In fact, I've already worked out a few suggestions and downloaded them onto a CD.'

He patted his pocket and smiled at Kirsten.

'I thought I could give you a look when we finish dinner. Do you have a computer in your flat?'

Josh knew full well that protecting Kirsten's fiancé from possible betrayal was way beyond his business, but telling himself it was for that reason and no other made his next statement easier.

'Great!' he said, with far more enthusiasm than he felt. 'I'll come up, too. After all, I'm seeing the Maintenance people in the morning, so it's best I have some idea of what's planned.'

The quick look of gratitude and relief Kirsten flashed him justified his decision, but he'd have felt happier inside himself if he'd believed her comfort, or the fiancé protection lark, was the only reason he was going to hang around.

But nothing was going to be easy. Nothing connected with Kirsten Collins ever was!

With dinner finished, they'd no sooner entered Kirsten's flat than the phone rang, and he had to listen to twenty minutes of her side of an obviously most satisfactory conversation with the fiancé. Actually, he needn't have listened to the conversation. He could have joined Matt at the computer in the far corner of the room and concentrated on the patterned screen Matt was manipulating.

But his ears had strained to hear words and, though mostly indistinct, they'd carried a carefree lilt of happiness that had made him, once again, wonder if he might be developing intestinal problems.

'Sorry,' she said, when she'd finished with a little glow of colour brushed across her cheeks, turning the tiny freckles a darker gold. 'But we've been missing each other the last few nights and needed to catch up.'

She crossed the room to lean over Matt at the computer, one hand resting lightly on his shoulder. Josh instantly regretted not showing more interest in the program, though to be wishing himself in Matt's place was sick, considering, even if she had been free, he didn't want to get involved with Kirsten.

Matt was talking about colour wheels and images and showing how a series of shapes could suddenly turn into a dinosaur when a particular colour was used to highlight the screen.

'That's the easiest of the manipulations. Changing the pictures by changing the colour of the entire screen. But for older kids, by selecting particular shapes then changing their colours, you can alter the picture altogether.'

He demonstrated, moving the mouse swiftly across the screen, selecting seemingly random shapes within the pattern. Then click, and a picture of a black-caped alien appeared, complete with a viciously spitting ray gun.

'Too complex?' Matt asked, and Kirsten shook her head.

'We've fourteen- and fifteen-year-olds still classed as "children" on the ward—this would be ideal for them as they begin to feel a little better.'

She straightened up, removing, to Josh's relief, her hand from Matt's shoulder, then said to Josh, 'I haven't had much time to read up on it, but they'll be extremely sick for a lot of the time, won't they?'

He saw the concern in her eyes, and irrationally wished it could be for him—then answered honestly.

'Very sick,' he confirmed. 'Total body irradiation affects all the body, but especially the lining of the intestine, so they are physically sick, and have diarrhoea. With a number of them, we'll probably have to use parenteral feeding, giving them nutrition in ways that bypass the alimentary canal, but they have to go back to real food eventually.'

They talked a while longer—about the programs Matt might be able to devise, about Kirsten's determination to get the equipment they'd need, and about the likelihood of the unit's success.

'I know that overall statistics are against us as far as saving all these kids is concerned, but any life saved is a triumph, isn't it?' Kirsten said.

'My thoughts exactly,' Josh told her, though he wasn't surprised at how in tune they were on the subject. Being in tune with Kirsten was one of the things that had prompted him to ask her out—that and being physically so attracted to her he hadn't been able to not ask her out.

'I'll leave you the CD so you can play with the program,' Matt was saying, as he shut down the computer and slid the CD into a protective box.

But Josh's attention was on Kirsten, caught by something that had passed between them in that moment of accord. It was as if an invisible beam had somehow joined them, attuning them to each other's thoughts and feelings.

He stepped towards her, certain the startled look in her eyes meant she, too, was feeling this strange epiphany—this oneness. Then the faint residual colour in her cheeks deepened and she moved away, fingering the ring she wore on her left hand.

'You'd better go,' she said, and he didn't argue, though he did make sure Matt left with him, chattering all the time about how great Kirsten was, and offering wagers to Josh about how soon he, Matt, could get her into bed.

'Oh, grow up, for heaven's sake, Matt!' Josh growled. 'The woman's engaged and even if she wasn't she wouldn't be interested in a rat-bag like you. She's looking for commitment—always has been.'

'Tried yourself, have you?' Matt teased, but Josh didn't deign to answer.

Though, damn it all, this nonsense between himself and Kirsten had to be resolved. Or maybe it wasn't between them—maybe, these days, she saw him as nothing more than a colleague. Maybe he was imagining this epiphany thing—and it was all one-sided, and nothing more than unrequited lust.

CHAPTER FIVE

BUT understanding the cause didn't lessen the effect. Josh arrived in Ward 6C the following morning to find Kirsten already there, talking to Jack Webster's parents about the preparatory regimen for Jack.

'The most likely source of infection in a person who's had total body irradiation which has killed off all the body's immunity to disease is the person themselves. The intestines are alive with bacteria that can cause terrible illnesses, and the skin itself sheds bacteria here, there and everywhere.'

For someone who hadn't had a lot of time to read the books he'd lent her, she wasn't doing too badly! And for that reason, and because there was something rather pleasant about watching her at work, her hands moving to illustrate points, her thick bell of hair swinging as she turned from one listener to the other, he let her talk.

'So Dr Phillips will prescribe antibiotics before treatment starts, and the nurses will be doing a lot of skin care.'

She broke off as the little boy, bored with the puzzle he'd been doing, joined them at a little table in the play area.

'I was telling your mum and dad about germs, Jack,' Kirsten said, leaning towards the child. 'And when you go into the special room to have your next lot of treatment, they'll both have to be very careful not to bring any germs into your room.'

'We need a germ ray gun,' Jack said, lifting his thin little arms to fire an imaginary gun.

'Or maybe we can make sure they always wear gowns and masks, and you watch from the bed so you know if they've washed their hands.'

He nodded, but the expression on his face said the ray gun would be better.

Josh stepped forward, shook Michael Webster's hand, then reached down to shake Jack's as well.

'Ready, champ?' he said to the little boy.

Jack nodded.

'You know what's going to happen?'

Again a confident nod, then Jack said, 'I'm going to have more treatment and get very sick and you're giving me some stuff from my sister Linda, then I'm still going to be sick a while but in the end I'll get better.'

If only I could promise that—be one hundred per cent sure, Josh thought. Glancing up, he saw Kirsten watching him and knew she knew exactly what he was thinking.

She excused herself and walked away, leaving him to discuss the actual treatment timetable with the Websters. As there was little time to waste, Jack's treatment would begin in one of the isolation rooms already available on the ward, with a combination of chemo drugs and total body irradiation to wipe out any existing malignancies, and antibiotics, anti-vomiting-and-nausea drugs added to the mix as required.

Kirsten pressed her hand to her chest, sure the exaggerated beating of her heart was due to concern over Jack's ultimate fate, not the expression in Josh's eyes when he'd looked at her across the top of the little boy's head.

We hope, it had said, as clearly as if he'd spoken the words, and the anguish it had prompted within Kirsten was for the man as well as for the child. Little Jack would die if the treatment failed, but Kirsten knew a little bit of Josh would die with him. And how many bits like that could one man afford to lose?

The pain she felt for him was even worse than the revelation when he'd held her after the accident—and her body had responded to him in ways an engaged body shouldn't. But hurting for him went far beyond physical attraction. Hurting for someone was all bound up in love, and she couldn't possibly be in love with Josh.

Attracted to him—yes. She'd known that from the first day they'd met. But love?

Impossible!

Love was serious stuff.

And surely was what she felt for Grant, or would feel as their relationship developed.

It wasn't what she felt for Josh.

So why was she hurting for him?

'Damn it all!' she muttered to herself as she walked into the tearoom to retrieve a new puzzle she'd found in the toy library the previous afternoon.

'Problems?'

She looked up, startled to find someone there, then grinned at Betty.

'I don't make a habit of talking to myself, but my head's telling me one thing and my heart's telling me another.'

'Want to talk about it?'

Kirsten was tempted, but she shook her head. She could have labelled the men A and B, but Betty was a perceptive woman and she'd soon work out who B was.

Gabi was the ideal confidante, but as her family was involved, she couldn't be expected to be impartial. Briefly, Kirsten considered phoning Alana up in 8B and asking her if they could meet for lunch, but Alana's life was so together she'd probably laugh, and almost certainly tell Kirsten to go with the flow—with more instinct and less reasoning.

Daisy Rutherford, who had the flat opposite Alana's, gave out advice to lovelorn teenagers as part of her internet chat room and radio talk-back programs, but Kirsten wasn't sure if the problem she was facing now would have been the same—back when she had been a fifteen-year-old.

Life had been simpler then, the options seemingly endless. At twenty-eight there were the limits imposed by maturity—which brought in its wake the compelling virtues of honesty and decency.

But also with maturity came responsibility, and she had a job to do. She shoved the problem into the back of her mind and picked up her notes on the patients currently in 6C. A little girl, Crystal, with whom she'd played the previous afternoon, had lost an eye to cancer and was having difficulty getting her hand-eye coordination back on track. Kirsten walked out to the nurses' station where she checked on a wall chart that Crystal wasn't scheduled for drug treatment today, then she found the things she'd need and crossed to where the ten-year-old was playing with a doll.

'Can you take her clothes off?' Kirsten asked. She held up a miniature blue ball dress. 'We could dress her in this—let her go to the ball, like Cinderella.'

'Cinderella's baby stuff, but Kylie wears dresses like that.'

'Kylie?' Kirsten echoed.

'Minogue—the singer. She's an Australian—did you know? I think she's just the best. Mum's getting me her latest CD and I've got a copy of her video and I watch it all the time. I can dance like her.'

Crystal stood up and swayed, in a parody of mature sexiness, to a tuneless hum. The doll, still partly clad, lay neglected on the floor.

Kirsten picked it up and waited until the dancing finished.

'Then let's dress her like Kylie,' she said to Crystal. 'You take this off while I see if there any high-heeled sandals to go with the ball gown.'

But though she shuffled through the bag of doll's clothes, her eyes were on the child, and the way her fingers fumbled with the buttons on the doll's dress.

What else interested ten-year-olds? They'd gone beyond the normal puzzles used to get much younger children to exercise their fine motor skills and develop coordination. What else was there?

'A jigsaw puzzle with Kylie Minogue on it?' The woman in the toy store repeated Kirsten's request, but put the world's biggest question mark after it. 'No, I'm sure we haven't, though the video store has a big poster from her latest album.'

A poster! Pasted on cardboard then cut. Better than a conventional jigsaw really, because Kirsten could manipulate the size and shape of the pieces.

She was walking back up the road from the shopping centre to the hospital, a rolled-up poster in one hand and a large sheet of stiff cardboard in the other, when a car pulled up beside her.

'Give you a lift?' Josh asked, and though she did briefly consider it, some aspects of her clothing—a slim-fitting knee-length skirt and high-heeled sandals—decided her.

'It's not far now. Easier to walk up to the front entrance

than make my way down from wherever you get a space in the parking tower out the back.'

Josh pretended to look shocked.

'My dear girl—I don't have to look for parking spaces, I have a reserved one right near the lift on the second floor.'

'Well, all power to you,' Kirsten said, 'but I'll still walk.'

She remembered maturity and manners.

'Thanks anyway!'

She walked on, lifting her rolled-up Kylie in salute as he roared past her, but escape wasn't going to be that easy. It was as if fate was throwing them together whenever possible.

'What on earth are they?' he asked, meeting her in the sixth-floor foyer and walking with her towards the ward.

'A Kylie poster and cardboard,' Kirsten said, for the sheer pleasure of thwarting him.

'Don't think I'm going to give you the satisfaction of asking what for!' Josh told her, then he gave her a hopeful smile and added, 'But you might just tell me anyway.'

'I'm making a jigsaw. For Crystal. She's a big Kylie fan.'

'So won't she object to you cutting her up?'

They'd reached the ward and Kirsten was about to head for the tearoom where she could spread out her finds, but the question halted her.

'Hell, I hadn't thought of that! I certainly hope not.' She frowned, tapping the poster against her thigh as she worried about this unforeseen consequence. 'But I'd better ask her.'

She dashed away and Josh smiled as he watched the long legs flash with each swift stride.

Kirsten's unpredictability might be maddening to whatever poor chap ended up marrying her, but it brought great delight to the children with whom she worked. It was one of the many qualities that made her so good at what she did.

Lateral thinking—that was her gift. Now, if he could set himself a bit of lateral thinking where Kirsten was concerned, it might blot out some of the more horizontal thoughts he kept on having.

CHAPTER SIX

IT WAS Arabella's mother, Pam Wilson, delighted to see Kirsten back on the ward, who talked her into going back on to the fund-raising committee.

'You're so good with corporate sponsors,' she said, when she'd insisted Kirsten lunch with her in the coffee-shop. No table service, though!

'As far as functions go,' Pam continued, 'we've got this Bush Dance coming up, but that's mostly a hospital thing. We need to get out into the wider community and there's so much competition for people's money.'

'Tell me about the Bush Dance,' Kirsten suggested, knowing she was far too muddled in her mind to be think-ing of good ideas for fund-raising functions right now.

So Pam prattled on, about costumes—everyone on the committee was coming as a famous country person—and ticket sales—not nearly enough sold—and decorations for the venue, which was the hospital gym.

'Surely all we need are some bales of straw and a lot of country-looking stuff—saddles and bridles and whips and cowboy hats,' Kirsten suggested. 'What else do they have in the country?'

Not the best of questions for someone engaged to a man from those parts to be asking, but she'd never got around to going further than the occasional picnic in the bush— in a civilised park on a mountaintop an hour's drive from the city.

'Horses?' Pam said, in a voice that told Kirsten she

knew even less about the parts that made up most of the Australian continent.

'I don't think horses dance,' Kirsten told her. 'Besides, one end bites and the other end kicks—and also makes indescribable messes on the floor if you're not careful. Let's rule out livestock of any kind as decorative features.'

In the end they decided to go down to the gym, which was normally used for rehab patients but could easily be cleared for parties and dances, so they could check out exactly what might go where.

'Trees—that's what we need to give it atmosphere. Who do we know with an acreage property on the edge of town, who won't mind us lopping off a few tree branches?'

'Josh.'

Pam said the name with such conviction it startled Kirsten.

'Josh Phillips? Our Josh? But he's a city boy, lives in that penthouse across the river from the hospital.'

'Only during the week,' Pam said, revealing how much more she knew about Josh than Kirsten, who'd actually dated him for a month. 'At weekends he usually goes out to the old family home. His mother still lives there and she's on her own now all the children have grown up and gone their separate ways.'

His mother still lived there? All alone? Kirsten wanted to ask where Dr Phillips—the father—lived, but it wasn't any of her business so she went with the other strange thing to come out of the conversation.

'Somehow Josh's car doesn't provide an image of a country boy.'

'Well, it's hardly country where his mother lives, but I remember him telling me there's a creek, and gum trees growing along it. He used to play there when he was a kid.'

Kirsten was forced to believe it, and also saddened to realise how little she knew of him—how much of himself he'd kept hidden from her. Obviously because she didn't matter—and never had. She'd been a diversion, nothing more. Another notch on his bedpost. Although she hadn't been a notch after all.

And it explained why, when she'd left his apartment that long-ago evening, infuriated by his calm insistence that the relationship had nowhere to go, he'd never contacted her again. Not socially. Not even professionally to suggest she stay on in the paediatric wards.

Though when Alex Graham had come back, Josh had come by a few times. It had been weird, almost as if he'd been looking for an excuse to see her...

Pam was looking at her as if expecting some further conversation, and with difficulty Kirsten put aside the pain and confusion this conversation had caused and thought back to what they'd been discussing. Trees!

'Will you ask him about trees?'

'Sorry, no can do,' Pam said easily. 'I'm taking my little sweetheart home this afternoon. And with her at home and the baby, we probably won't even make it to the dance. Though we've bought tickets just in case. I'll give them to someone else if we can't make it.'

She went on, talking about the women who'd already been organised to help with the preparations.

'I'll get Jill to get the straw and other bibs and bobs. You'd remember Jill—her son Peter had ALL but went into remission after the first treatment and is still, touch wood, doing well. And there's a group of student nurses Betty has organised to help decorate on Saturday morning.

So if you could ask Josh about the trees, and if you can get them there by early afternoon, it'd be great.'

She went on to detail what else had been organised, who was in charge of seeing the band was paid, who was looking after the catering staff and who was on the door.

'Joy's in overall charge on the night. Make yourself known to her, but there's really nothing for you to do but organise trees and enjoy yourself—and sell some extra tickets if you can. But the next function—well, we'll all expect some big ideas.'

Pam breezed off, leaving Kirsten staring at the huge space they needed to turn into something vaguely resembling a barn with the aid of some straw and a few trees.

If Josh agreed to knocking down some trees...

'You don't need whole trees, just branches. I'm staying in town Friday night, so how about I pick you up at six on Saturday morning and we both go out and find a trailer-load of suitable stuff? Then I can drop it and you back, maybe give you a hand tying it up.'

Kirsten wasn't sure what shocked her more—the mentioned ETD, or a trailer-load of trees behind Josh's sporty black beast. And by the time she'd worked out that the 'six o'clock' arrangement was by far the most important issue and definitely needed to be addressed, he'd breezed away.

'Six o'clock!' she complained to Alana later, when they'd met in the corridor near the staff exit and were walking home together. 'Who on earth gets up at six o'clock?'

Alana chuckled. 'I was going to say farmers, but most of them get up much earlier than that. They go more on daylight than clocks and if the sun comes up at five, that's when they're ready to start work.'

Kirsten shuddered, then, thinking of her fiancé—which was a change from thinking about Josh—she said, 'Do wives have to get them breakfast, or are they well trained enough to get their own? I don't function too well in the mornings.'

Alana, who didn't need to be told about Kirsten's reluctance to leave her bed before the sun was well and truly doing its bit to brighten the world, simply smiled.

'You'll work it out,' she said. 'How is Grant, by the way? And when do you expect him down?'

Kirsten felt warmth spreading through her at the thought of the man with whom she'd clicked immediately. OK, so he didn't raise goose-bumps on her arms, but there was more to life than goose-bumps. In fact, going through life all be-goose-bumped would probably be most uncomfortable.

And distracting in the extreme.

'He's wonderful,' she told Alana, and meant it. 'Last night when he phoned, he said he'd try to get down for the Bush Dance at the weekend, but as it doesn't seem likely, he'll probably come in a month.'

She glanced at her friend. Should she mention the problem she was having with her skin still reacting to Josh? And that 'hurting for him' sensation which had all but floored her yesterday?

Better not, given that Alana had been a friend of Gabi's from forever, and no doubt would feel some loyalty to Grant.

The week passed quickly, young Jack undergoing his initial treatment, Crystal's co-ordination improving—though now she was due to go home, Kirsten had to devise a new set of games and exercises she could take with her to help her develop new skills.

A patient Kirsten hadn't known before, Michael

McKenna, had been admitted. Though in remission after his initial treatment, he'd caught an infection that was hard to shift and Josh had hospitalised him so stronger antibiotics could be used.

The four-year-old was restricted to his bed while antibiotics dripped into his veins, but he wasn't sick enough to lie still and when the television bored him Kirsten had to find other ways to keep him happy.

Drawing worked, and once she'd set up a board across his bed and provided him with an array of coloured pencils, he could lie, propped on pillows, and draw to his heart's content.

But it was the drawings themselves that interested Kirsten. Though crude representations of trees, flowers and grass, they had a magical quality, as if the viewer were being drawn into another world.

'He's drawn those same pictures since he came out of hospital after his first treatment,' his mother told Kirsten. 'He says it's a special place he found while he was in here.'

Kirsten understood. Counselling staff working with the children would often suggest they find a place inside their heads where they could go when everything felt really bad, but Kirsten had never seen such a 'place' depicted.

She found herself drawn back to Michael, studying the different drawings he did each day, seeing tiny birds and insects among the plants, imagining, perhaps, more than was actually there. It made her rethink the idea of patterned walls. Perhaps one room could have this glade...

'But this is it! This is Michael's glade. What a magic place.'

She turned to Josh, her delight and excitement so strong he must surely see it glowing out of her.

'What *are* you talking about?' Josh demanded, looking around the pleasant enough area by the creek where he and his brothers had played when they were young.

It looked the same to him, but something about it had transformed Kirsten from a cross—'This is uncivilised, going anywhere at this hour!'—reproachful and all but silent companion into this buzzingly alive creature, glowing with delight as she spun around and around, her arms held wide, marvelling at a bit of bushland with mist off the creek still wreathing through it.

And if he'd been regretting agreeing to this stupid idea before he'd picked her up—tree-felling on a day that already promised to be too crowded with other duties—he'd regretted it even more once he'd pulled up outside her building and Kirsten had climbed into the car, bringing with her a faint cloud of perfumed air—not too strong, but alluring.

Even brooding and pouting over the injustice of being up so early, she was as distracting as ever. More distracting in fact, as her 'tree-felling' gear was a pair of skin-tight pants that ended mid-calf and a little cropped top that left a lightly tanned midriff and a teasingly decorated belly button exposed to his gaze.

And it was no good telling himself not to look. As well tell a magnet not to pick up iron filings.

So he stood in 'Michael's glade' and looked at her, the comet that had zoomed back into his life. And try as he may to tell himself she wasn't for him, he had to admit that, seeing her here, where he'd played so often, she fitted right in.

'And this is it, just like the place he draws in pictures— the place he goes to when things get too bad,' she was saying, and with difficulty he guessed at what he'd missed.

'I know the therapists talk to the kids about going to a special place. I do it myself at times. You're saying he's actually depicted the place? A place like this?'

Kirsten nodded, her face alight with wonder and delight.

'Isn't it incredible? If you talk about special places, might you ever have described this?'

Josh shook his head, then shrugged.

'I talk about special places, but I don't know that I would describe this particular area. When I picture somewhere special myself, it's usually a mountaintop, looking down a valley between more mountains, and a lot of sky.'

And sometimes a woman with red-brown hair and long slender limbs, running across the grass to greet me—but he didn't tell her that part.

'Good for Michael being able to draw his place,' he added, wanting to get things out of dreams and back to practical reality. 'But right now we've got to get some branches for your decorations.'

'*Our* decorations. This is your unit too,' Kirsten reminded him.

She was disappointed by the shift in the mood between them, but at least that was better than the state of almost constant surprise she'd been in since he'd picked her up. Firstly, there'd been the drive—not out along the motorway in the direction of the trendy acreage suburbs, but north through less than salubrious dwellings, then onto a dirt road that wound up a small mountain, eventually turning into a property that had a big old rambling house, with cleared paddocks around it, but rampant bush, as dense and thick as prison walls, beyond these paddocks.

At the house, he'd disappeared briefly inside, then come back with keys, leading her towards a large shed and opening the door of an old but very serviceable Range

Rover for her. A trailer was already hitched on behind it, so someone had either got it ready for Josh, or it was there permanently, no doubt for shifting things about the property. They'd driven down to the creek in it, parked and walked into the glade.

Now he led her along a path away from the creek to where the trees grew taller and were less densely packed, their lower branches bending towards the ground.

'I thought I could lop off some of these. If you think they'll be OK, I can drive around through another paddock so we won't have to lug them very far.'

Kirsten nodded. As far as she could tell, branches off these trees would be ideal. But the experience in the glade by the creek had unsettled her. No, driving out to this place with Josh, seeing the big house hidden away in the bush—that's what had unsettled her. The glade had merely deepened the feeling until now she was so edgy she was afraid to open her mouth, fearful of what questions she might blurt out.

'Do you want to wait here, or come with me? I have to drive back up towards the house, then around through a couple of paddocks to get close.'

'I'll wait here,' she said, and watched him walk away.

So why did we come this way? That was one question that she *could* have asked, but she hadn't. Surely not because she preferred to think Josh wanted her to see that magic place?

She wandered down towards the creek, kneeling by the bank and scooping the clear cold water into her hands—splashing it across her face. Droplets, splashing back in, distorted the reflections, making trees shimmer and the blue sky break into a ripple effect. She waited until the water stopped moving and the reflection became clear again, then splashed first one part, then another, seeing the ripple effect and watching how the picture changed.

She was hoping to get changing pictures to help sick children through their treatment, but the ripple effect of this new involvement with Josh—where would that end? What picture would that change?

Lost in thought, she failed to hear the vehicle, or he'd parked so far away she might not have heard it anyway. But suddenly he was there, kneeling beside her, watching the images blur then renew themselves.

'In my memory, I spent most of my childhood by this creek,' he said quietly, taking out a handkerchief and wiping first one of her hands, then the other. 'I know I went to school, and we had holidays at the beach, so sometimes I think maybe you remember the really happy times more vividly, so it seems as if I was always by the creek.'

His task finished, he'd kept hold of her hands, and though she willed them to move away, Kirsten found they'd lost the ability to act, so she knelt, her hands in Josh's, and heard sadness in a voice that spoke of happy memories. How or why they ended up kissing was something, later, she couldn't fathom. Had he started it? She?

Not that it mattered, because the kiss was like coming home. She was in Josh's arms and he was kissing her as frantically as she was kissing him, then, with their arms wound tightly around each other, they were lying on the grassy bank, drinking in the very essence of each other like thirst-maddened wanderers finally reaching an oasis.

His lips explored, entreated, teased, and hers responded, matching his explorations, begging and teasing, feeling a degree of satisfaction yet a deep-felt need for more.

And when kissing was no longer enough, when Josh's hand slid under her top, caressing her breast, and her hand sought out his body, sliding below the waistband of his jeans, a wild elation ripped through Kirsten's body and she wanted to shout her pleasure to the sky.

Satiny skin rippled beneath her fingers, soft strands of hair flattening at her touch, his heat burning into her, as hers must surely be burning into him. She slipped a button open, reached for a zip—

Damn! Something had snagged on the heavy material, halting her questing fingers. What…?

She sat up, turning away from him, clutching her left hand in her right as if the ring itself might somehow be shamed by what she had done.

Josh moved more slowly, his eyes on her face, a million questions in the blueness.

'It's no use,' she said to him, shaking her head as she tried to deny what she was about to admit. 'Whatever it is between us isn't going to go away just because we want it to. Unless we have—' somehow 'sex' seemed too raw a word though that was undoubtedly all it would be '—that physical relationship.'

Josh looked startled, but obviously grasped the content, for his hand moved towards her and she knew, within seconds, she'd be back in his arms.

She leapt to her feet, moving more from temptation than from the man who offered it.

'Not yet,' she said, then laughed ruefully and shook her head again. 'No, it's not a "not yet" like last time—like my month-long embargo. This is a serious not yet, Josh. A "not until I'm unengaged" not yet. I've got to do that first. Tell Grant. Be free. I couldn't cheat, couldn't do that. Do you understand?'

No! Not any of it, Josh could have said, but something so blunt might have destroyed the delicate balance that had apparently manifested itself between them. What he did understand was that he was finally—and hopefully before too long—going to get Kirsten into his bed. He was going to make love to his flaming, erratic comet and get all the fantasies, and his father's dire warning, out of his system once and for all.

'Do we have a timetable for this plan? This unengagement?'

It sounded cold and callous, but it needed to be said.

Green eyes, so troubled it took all his strength not to take her in his arms again, looked appealingly into his.

'He should be down soon. Or maybe I can phone—or write...'

The words dropped hesitantly into the air between them and he knew she was already hurting for the man he didn't know.

Already regretting the decision?

No! She was too honest and straight-down-the-line to play games like that, but he sure as hell was mucking up her life.

And the other man's...

But for all the troubled shadows in her eyes, the cool, practical Phillips voice in his head took the opportunity to point out that this was further proof why a woman like Kirsten was such utterly unsuitable wife material.

Breaking off an engagement with one man because of a physical attraction to another?

For sex with another, to put it bluntly?

Not good!

'Perhaps we'd better cut down some trees,' he said abruptly, and heard Kirsten sigh.

Had she expected him to be more romantic?

He strode away—from the idea and from her—assuming she'd follow.

She hadn't been romantic about it, he reminded himself, justifying both his acceptance of her decision and the

manner in which he'd finished the discussion. She'd made
it sound like some contract she was about to undertake.
And she knew the rules—well, his rule about no future.
So romance didn't really come into it.

But apparently, like him, she'd reached the stage where
she couldn't go forward into her own future until this
attraction between them had been squared away.

He was walking back to where he'd left the chainsaw
as he considered all of this, then he realised she wasn't
following. He turned and saw her kneeling by the creek,
where she'd been when he'd returned earlier. And seeing
her there, her fingers trailing dreamily in the water, her
thick hair swinging forward to hide her face, he felt a jab
of deep sadness in the region of his heart, as if the affair
were already over and they were parted, and nothing remained but his memories.

Which were fickle things at best—just look at the way
he felt about the creek!

Kirsten knew she should follow, but if she'd expected
happiness to erupt within her now she'd made a decision,
she was sadly disappointed.

Not that she *had* expected happiness. Relief, perhaps?
A certain excitement? But all she felt was nothing.

Perhaps her emotions had shut down—or been put on
hold—until she spoke to Grant. And that was difficult. By
rights, she'd have preferred to have done it in person
rather than over the phone—definitely not by email. But
if she wouldn't be seeing him for a month…

Or perhaps it was because she knew it had no future,
but had realised she could no longer hold out against the
attraction she felt for Josh. So she'd be going into the
very kind of relationship she'd always sworn she wouldn't
have. Hell, her month-long-embargo had grown out of

distaste for so-called 'flings'. Get to know the man first, she'd decided, then see where she wanted to go with him.

A well-planned, sensible course.

Until Josh Phillips had entered her life!

She left the creek, and walked towards the loud rumble of a machine—no doubt, cutting branches off a tree. Sadness walked beside her, as if the brief affair were already over before it had begun and she was feeling the pain she knew the future held for her.

Josh stopped for long enough to tell her to stay clear, then started the big saw again, moving from tree to tree until it looked as if a whole mini-forest had been felled.

'OK, now we load them,' he said, grabbing a branch and dragging it towards the trailer.

How romantic! Kirsten wanted to say, but she knew this time she'd made the rules—and the first move—so she could hardly ask for romance.

They worked together, loading the branches, then with a coil of blue and yellow rope from the back of the Range Rover Josh tied them down.

'I've more rope there—what else do we need?' he asked, and she looked at him, wondering how he could be just the way he'd been before they'd kissed.

Before she'd made the momentous decision.

But why wouldn't he be? After all, he didn't have an engagement he had to break, a fiancé he had to hurt. He was getting what he'd wanted all along, with no risk to his plans, or his emotions.

If he had any…

She shot a glance at him, and realised he was waiting for her to answer him.

'I can't think of anything,' she said, and saw him smile and move a little closer.

'No?' he murmured, but he made no further move, just

stood there, within touching—kissing—distance, making her heart pound with the excitement of wanting him and her head hurt with the ramifications of what she was about to do.

'No!' she said firmly, and turned away from him, aware that she had to talk to Grant as soon as possible. If she delayed and Josh continued to play these games whenever they were together, she'd go screaming mad from frustration.

Talking work helped, and when they reached the hospital a dozen nurses were running around with straw bales and country paraphernalia so she was safe from more distractions—or distracted enough to be safe from her own desires.

'Thanks,' she said to Josh, when he'd finished tying up the branches, now standing up against pillars and walls and looking more like trees. 'I know you've got a ward round to do, so we can finish up here.'

He hesitated but in the end he walked away with nothing more than, 'See you later, then.' Kirsten wondered about that hesitation, then with a heavy heart guessed what it might have meant.

According to hospital gossip, Josh was rarely without a woman in his life. So, no doubt, he'd intended bringing the present incumbent in that role to the dance tonight. He'd hesitated over whether he should explain this to Kirsten—or just arrive with someone like Roberta Smythe, whose social pedigree was as flawless as the Phillipses' medical one.

Not that someone with a fiancé of her own required such an explanation...

Jill had arranged sandwiches to be delivered from the canteen, so Kirsten and the other helpers worked through lunchtime, finally, at four, agreeing that the gym looked as good as it would ever look. Tired and dusty, she made her way home.

To find two surprises.

One was hovering in the doorway of the other flat on the fourth floor, obviously waiting for her return. Six feet three, and all muscle, he ignored her exclamations of surprise and swept her into his arms for a hearty kiss. Not quite the moment to tell him she didn't want to be engaged to him any more. Then Gabi appeared. She'd been delegated to hire a costume for Kirsten, and the plastic suit-bag in her hand suggested she'd done just that. Even found a hat, if the hatbox in her other hand was any indication.

'I know you'll probably shriek,' she told Kirsten, with a smile at her brother that suggested he already knew what was going on, 'but there wasn't much left in your size. You could have been a chorus girl from an old Wild West saloon, but the fishnet stockings had big holes in them— or you could be Dolly.'

She passed the hatbox and suit-bag to Kirsten then, turning to her brother, said, 'And don't you laugh. I got you a country-and-western-style shirt and a huge hat to go with it.'

'Hey,' he protested. 'I'm a country boy. I was going to go as myself.'

Kirsten ignored the banter, stuck in a track of her own.

Dolly?

Dolly Parton?

'Dolly Parton's blonde!' she protested, and Gabi smiled.

Hoping she wouldn't find what she thought she'd find, Kirsten opened the hat-box. Inside was a blonde wig— definitely Dolly Parton.

She smiled at Gabi who was watching her in trepidation.

'OK, I'll go along with this,' she told her friend, 'but while the wig might help as far as hair is concerned, I haven't got her other attributes.'

Gabi laughed and excused herself, reminding Kirsten that a group of Near West tenants were meeting at Mickey's at six for an early meal before going on to the dance.

Alone with Grant, Kirsten wondered what to say. Grant solved the problem momentarily by kissing her again. But when the kiss left her feeling uneasy rather than elated, she knew she had to tell him.

But right now?

Or should she leave it until after the dance?

Let him enjoy himself first? After all, he'd obviously flown down especially for it.

A second kiss decided the matter. How could she kiss Grant while her body lusted after Josh?

She pulled out of his arms, and looked up into his rugged face, smiling lips and sparkling eyes.

'You're going to tell me I rushed you into this engagement, aren't you?' he said. 'Well, I did, and that's done but I'm not going to rush you any more. We can take all the time we want before we get married. And I'm not going to listen to anything negative you have to say about it.'

'Not going to listen?' Kirsten repeated. 'What do you mean, you're not going to listen?'

'Just that,' he said, almost smugly, as he bent and kissed her again.

'But it isn't a matter of time. I want to give you back

the ring. I should never have accepted it in the first place,' she protested, dodging away from the approaching lips and struggling to pull the ring off her finger. Of course, after all the work she'd been doing, her fingers had swollen and the ring wasn't going anywhere.

'See, it won't come off, which proves it's meant to be,' Grant said calmly. 'And even if you do get it off, I won't take it back, and if you don't wear it you'll probably lose it, or have it stolen, and it's quite valuable, you know.'

Kirsten stopped struggling with the piece of jewellery and stared, bemused, at the man who'd given it to her.

'B-but that's the w-way people break engagements,' she stuttered. 'The woman gives back the ring. You have to take it.'

'Some other time, maybe,' Grant said easily, smiling at her as if she were a recalcitrant child. 'I bet this is all because you're hungry. Gabi's still got some of Mum's Christmas cake at her place. I'll duck in and get us some.'

'I don't want Christmas cake,' Kirsten told his departing back, but something told her he would ignore that statement as easily as he'd ignored her attempts to break off the engagement.

He returned with a tray containing not only Christmas cake but a plate of biscuits, cheese and fruit as well.

'There, you have a nibble at this while you shower and get dressed. You've no idea how much better you'll feel.'

Kirsten doubted it. What she actually felt was as if the top of her head were about to explode.

'I *won't* feel better until we've sorted this out,' she shrieked at him, then realised her voice was probably carrying across the foyer to Gabi and Alex's flat.

But she didn't want to shut her door with Grant still on this side of it.

'Which we'll do,' he said, putting his hand on her shoulder with the lightest of touches. 'All in good time. I promise.'

He smiled as if that was his last word on the subject, and Kirsten, realising she might as well argue with the door, shook her head and grabbed a piece of cake.

'I'm going to have a shower,' she muttered, then realised she was, in fact, obeying his instructions—eating cake, taking a shower, wearing the ring—but not feeling better at all.

She turned back towards him and tried again.

'There's someone else,' she said, and though she sensed a flicker of movement in his body, there was no obvious reaction to her blunt words.

'Are you going to marry him?'

The question shook her, and she answered automatically.

'No!'

'Good. Then we can stay engaged.'

'While I have an affair with someone else?'

Disbelief raised her voice about twenty-seven octaves and she wondered again just how much the Grahams might be hearing.

'Do you love him?'

Kirsten hesitated.

'No. It's just something I have to get out of my system.'

'I can handle that,' Grant said, so calmly Kirsten began to wonder if she was dreaming. 'I can wait.'

Again Kirsten couldn't find the words she needed, not

immediately. And when they did come, they were so faint, so hesitant, it was a wonder he heard them.

'No, that's not fair either,' she whispered. 'Because though that's how it will be, an affair and an ending, I'm afraid it mightn't end for me, and all I'd be offering you was what was left—not second best exactly, but not a whole heart either.'

He took her in his arms and held her close, so she could feel the beating of his heart against his chest wall. His hand stroked her hair, a gentle giant, comforting *her* when she was the one causing pain.

'You even sound confused,' he said softly, 'which proves I'm right. So take your time, wear the ring, especially tonight so we don't have to explain anything to Gabi and Alex, then have your fling with this other chap and let the future take care of itself.'

He eased her away and smiled down at her.

'*Now* go and have that shower. You're the grubbiest woman I've held in my arms for a long time!' He smiled. 'We'll live for the moment. And since I've flown in especially to take you to the dance, let's make tonight a night to remember.'

She didn't respond to that suggestion—she had an awful feeling what it might be like with Grant and Josh in the same room—but did head for the shower, although her movements were slow, her feet dragging, as if her floor were suddenly thick with treacle.

Had she broken off her engagement?

She'd certainly told Grant in every possible way she could that it was over, even if he had refused to listen.

Was there such a thing as a one-sided engagement?

Damn the man—what was wrong with him? Why

couldn't he have been upset, or jealous, or flown into a towering rage, like any normal man?

Though once she got the ring off—and gave it back— then surely everything would be OK.

And whatever happened, he was right about tonight. He'd flown down because she'd asked him to accompany her to the dance—at least she could make an effort to see he enjoyed himself.

While the 'night to remember' aspect of it all was virtually assured—one way or another.

CHAPTER SEVEN

IT WAS certainly going to be a night to remember, Kirsten realised when she eventually pulled the Dolly Parton dress over her head and tugged to adjust it around her body. It was made of soft golden suede, with long tassels dangling across the yoke at the back, from pockets on the top and right around the hem of the very minimal skirt. But it was the top that worried her more than the skirt length.

Some engineering feat in the construction of the bodice meant her quite satisfactory though not over-abundant breasts had taken on the look of Dolly's most startling attributes. And try as she may to tug the neckline higher, or to persuade some of the leather tassels to fall across what seemed like acres of bulging breast-flesh, nothing changed. She was going to have to spoil the fun of the party by not dressing up, or go along with an eye-catching cleavage that would be the talk of the hospital for months.

'At least you have the wig. No one will know who you are,' Gabi said, when, caught between despair and disaster, Kirsten dashed across the foyer to demand help.

'But look at me,' Kirsten wailed. 'I'm practically indecent.'

'Nonsense! I find it extremely attractive.'

Alex had joined them and, while not exactly ogling Kirsten's over-revealed chest, he had certainly taken note of it.

Then Grant appeared in a red satin shirt with silver braid on it.

His eyes, too, were drawn to Kirsten's problem.

'Mmm. Nice!'

Kirsten took a swing at him.

'This isn't funny! I'm supposed to be in costume.'

'You *are* in costume,' Gabi pointed out. 'And they don't look vulgar. Just not like you.'

'Are they false?' Grant asked, and Kirsten resisted the urge to hit him again. Then she realised he was trying to help and shook her head.

'It's some kind of structural engineering in the top. Someone as flat as a pancake would probably look the same. I'll have to wear a jacket—or a cardigan—cover them up.'

Grant took her hand.

'No way! I'm going there looking like a goose in this shirt, and you look absolutely gorgeous. If it bothers you, just keep dancing. I'll hold you close and no one need see.'

'Well, I'll wear a jacket there and back,' Kirsten said, 'even though it's been hot enough today to fry eggs on the pavement, and it's not likely to be much cooler to-night.'

She went back inside for a jacket, checked she had the tickets, then met Gabi, Alex and Grant in the foyer.

Down at Mickey's, Graham and Madeleine Frost, who had the penthouse on the top floor, were already settled at a table, and Alana had just joined them. Gabi introduced Grant to the Frosts, explaining to him that Graham was also a doctor at Royal Westside, then everyone settled into chairs.

Which brought Kirsten, who'd been not exactly hiding behind Grant but certainly keeping out of sight, into view.

When she'd had enough of the ribald comments about the neckline and had fielded half a dozen 'blonde' jokes, Kirsten turned the conversation to other matters.

'I tried to talk Daisy into coming, but she's got some special programme on tonight—doing a street crawl interviewing youngsters who should probably be at home in bed. And Marg on the third floor is on duty.'

Speaking of other medically related tenants prompted Gabi to ask Madeleine, whose father owned the building, about the new arrivals on the first and third floors.

'I've only met the dentists on the first floor a couple of times,' Madeleine told her, 'and the fellow who had taken the other flat on three can't take it right now so it's vacant at the moment.'

She glanced around the group.

'Do you know anyone who's looking for a place?'

'I heard someone talking about a new specialist physician,' Alex said. 'Someone just back from a stint overseas. I'll ask around and if I can track him down, mention the building.'

'If it's Rory Forrester, don't bother!' Alana said. 'He's the original disappearing man. So far, no one's set eyes on him, but the shock waves of his arrival have been spreading.'

There was enough bite in Alana's voice to surprise Kirsten, as the nurse was usually super-cool. But right now she wanted to get the conversation off medical matters—after all, Grant was here as a favour to her and she didn't want him bored stiff before they even reached the dance.

She might not want to be engaged to him, but he certainly deserved her consideration!

She switched the conversation to the party ahead of them, thanking them all for buying tickets and making an effort to dress up. Then it was time to order, and a discussion of food and wine took over at the far end of the table. Alex asked Grant how the shearing had gone, and the technical conversation that followed between Gabi and Grant over the fineness of the wool kept Grant happy down this end.

Which left Kirsten free to think, for the first time today, of the commitment she'd made to Josh.

Could you call agreeing to a brief affair a commitment?

And was she mad to have even suggested it?

But surely something was better than nothing?

She rubbed her thumb across the inner band of her engagement ring—that had to be sorted out as well. Perhaps because she'd been tired she hadn't explained things clearly to Grant. She'd try again in the morning.

The thought made her sigh.

Grant's arm came round her shoulders and he gave her a quick hug. He was so aware of how she was feeling—wasn't that worth saving?

She hadn't really given him a fair go, given the engagement a chance...

'You can't sort it out overnight,' he murmured, leaning close so only she would hear the words. 'So stop fretting and live for the moment.'

'Repeating a silly cliché like that doesn't make things any easier,' she snapped, guilt making her edgy.

'No?' he said, and smiled, and she decided she'd try to go along with it, nodding reluctantly and concentrating on her meal.

They walked to the hospital, a loose group with the configurations of twos and threes changing several times. The oohs and aahs of surprise when they saw the decorated gym was very gratifying to Kirsten, and after a glass of wine and a lively dance with Grant, she relaxed enough to forget her problems with her cleavage and begin to enjoy herself.

Until she danced past Josh and saw his scowl, which

deepened as they drew close enough for him to see more of her than he usually did.

Except for that one time!

'So that's the man,' Grant murmured, surprising Kirsten with his perception. Then he drew her closer and added, 'I definitely won't give you up for him. He looks a bad-tempered brute and you deserve the best.'

He was joking, or she hoped so, but she did notice that whenever they happened, in future dances, to gravitate anywhere near Josh, Grant always held her closer.

'Now you're back on the committee, you'd better come and meet the rest of us.'

Jill Clarke, who'd been in charge of straw bales and the general decorating, grabbed Kirsten as the band stopped for a break.

Gabi excused herself and followed Jill towards a table at the far end of the room. Two tables, in fact—the first with members of the fund-raising committee and the second with an impressive collection of senior staff including a full roll call of Phillipses. The old man, Dr Harold, sat at one end; two other men Kirsten vaguely recognised as Josh's brothers were either side of him, with austerely attractive women seated by *their* sides. None had made the slightest concession to the 'bush' theme, though Josh, at the far end, opposite his father, was in jeans and a checked shirt, with a worn and sensible wide-brimmed hat, much beloved of Australian bushmen, hanging from the back of his chair.

Kirsten nodded to him as she followed Jill to the committee's table, and though her hands positively throbbed with the need to pull her dress higher, she wasn't willing to draw even more attention to her neckline.

At the fund-raisers' table, Kirsten greeted women she'd met earlier in the day, then was introduced to their partners and finally to an older woman, elegantly dressed as a pioneer woman of the west. Joy someone, the surname lost as the members of the bush band tuned up their fiddles once again.

Joy patted a vacant seat beside her.

'Come and sit a minute. I know you've been dancing since you arrived.' She grinned at Kirsten. 'I couldn't help but notice you. Dolly's one of my favourite singers.'

'She's the last person I'd have thought of being,' Kirsten admitted. 'I left it up to a friend to get a costume for me.' Feeling safer now she was seated, she gave the bodice a hitch upward. 'Some friend!'

Joy chuckled then said, 'Oh, I don't know. I think you're carrying it off extremely well. People see far more flesh on the beach—why, most of the young women go topless there. And as for television...even the ads are becoming close to X-rated.'

'I know what you mean,' Kirsten said. 'I rarely watch it—I'd prefer to read—but I saw one the other day...'

They talked of ads and of books they enjoyed, books for light relief and books that made them think.

'I read a mix of both,' Kirsten admitted. 'With me it's a mood thing. Do I want escapism or something I can get my teeth into?'

Josh walked past at that moment and, presumably hearing her words, raised an eyebrow, but in spite of the eyebrow, he was still scowling so she ignored him.

'Poor Josh.' Joy's soft exclamation claimed all Kirsten's attention.

'Why poor Josh?' she demanded. 'After all, he's just got the unit he's been wanting, with this committee working to keep it in the public eye. He's adored by all his patients, by their parents and by the staff who work with him. What more could a dedicated doctor want?'

Joy turned to Kirsten.

'Nothing, I suppose. Certainly that's all my husband wanted—a successful career. Oh, he wanted children but that was a dynastic thing, continuing the line and all that rubbish. But—what's the expression they use now? He got off—is that right? He got off on the power and on the adulation of those around him. On being a kind of god, omnipotent.'

Kirsten didn't hide her surprise.

'But no doctor is omnipotent,' she protested.

Joy smiled faintly.

'No, of course they're not, but that doesn't stop some thinking they are.'

'Josh doesn't!' Kirsten said, stoutly defending the man in spite of the scowls—or was she defending the doctor, not the man?

Joy's smile was brighter this time.

'No, he doesn't, does he?' Then the smile faded and she added, 'But that doesn't stop him worrying that one day he'll turn into his father.'

Oh!

Kirsten looked more intently at the woman. She had short, greying hair which could once have been brown. Her eyes were also brown, not vivid blue, and her features were nothing like Josh's. Yet now Kirsten studied her, there was something there—maybe the carriage, the tilt of the head or the breadth of brow.

'You're his mother? Heavens, I could have been saying all kinds of terrible things about him.'

'I wouldn't have let you,' Joy said, patting Kirsten's hand. 'And I thought you'd know.'

Why the hell would I know? Kirsten wanted to shout. He certainly didn't bother to introduce me when I was out at your place earlier today.

And why—?

No, damn it all, she'd ask the next question out loud.

'Why aren't you at the other table—with your family?'

The brown eyes darkened with a kind of sadness.

'Being on the fund-raising committee makes it easy for me to still be part of Josh's success without actually joining in a grand Phillip's appearance. While the children were growing up—in fact, until they were all established in their careers—I came along to functions and stood by my husband's side, entertaining when asked, playing the dutiful wife. But now?'

She shrugged her scarf-draped shoulders.

'I won't pretend any more. I thought I could do it—that I could bring up my children so they never felt the lack of a father's love and presence—and I thought I'd succeeded. But I look at the older two and realise I've failed. They're replicas of their father and are following in his footsteps. Dutiful wives, beautifully presented children, to all appearances a perfect life, but Brad's wife drinks and Harry's wife has a succession of lovers. It's no wonder Josh is terrified of marriage—and also terrified of hurting someone the way he suspects I was hurt.'

The words were like shards of ice piercing Kirsten's heart. Listening to this unhappy woman, she could follow Josh's thought processes. He loved children—a blind man could have seen that much—but he had the double curse of a job that would often take him from his home after normal working hours so his children would be denied a lot of his time—his company—and the examples of his father and brothers as total failures in the happy families department.

Joy talked on about other things—the horses she bred, the life she'd made for herself—but Kirsten only half listened because, in her heart of hearts, she'd been ignoring Josh's repeated warnings that their affair wouldn't last.

Foolishly, somewhere inside her had dwelt a tiny bud of hope, and within its tightly furled leaves she'd packed a dream of happy ever after, and for ever and ever, and all the other phrases used to end the best romantic stories.

'Dance, Dolly?'

The subject of her thoughts had materialised beside her. He reached out, took her left hand and ran his thumb across the ring.

She retrieved her hand and didn't bother to tell him that, as far as she was concerned, the ring was making its final appearance.

Though Grant's behaviour was another worry...

'No,' she said, though the usual tremors his presence caused made it hard to deny him. 'I've left Grant to the mercy of all the single women here tonight for quite long enough.'

She excused herself to Joy and walked away, oblivious now of the revealing costume, because these new insights into the man she suspected she loved were outweighing all other considerations.

Josh watched her sashay off, then returned to his table in time to hear Harry's wife declaring, in her cool, well-bred tones, that she didn't know what the hospital was coming to, when staff could dress like that at an official fund-raising function.

'It's *supposed* to be fancy dress,' Josh told her, and heard his other sister-in-law titter.

'Fancy dress for a fancy lady—isn't that what they used to be called in the Wild West?'

Punching either of his female in-laws would be considered bad taste, but Josh didn't have to sit and listen to their bitchy nonsense. He excused himself and crossed to his mother's table, asking her to dance and refusing to accept any excuses.

'Did Grandfather's wife and the other in-laws always make you feel uncomfortable?' he asked her, as they whirled slowly around the edges of the crowd. 'Is that why you opted out of Dad's social life as soon as you felt you'd done your duty?'

'Your father opted out of my life, Josh, not me out of his. And, really, while I might have been intimidated by them early on, as I grew older I felt more sorry for all my in-laws.' She grinned at her son. 'Because they had to live with Phillips men.'

'Very comforting!' Josh said, but no matter how hard he tried he couldn't picture Kirsten, even not in Dollymode, sitting at the Phillips table.

Though it was alarming he should even try!

At midnight, the band played its final bracket, and almost before the last guests had departed, the cleaners moved in. They were there voluntarily so no one argued as they ushered the lingerers out the door.

Kirsten's group walked around the building, through the spacious hospital grounds, heading for the road that would take them home. The night was quiet, and for a time at least no sirens split the silence. They drifted along through the soft air, reliving the evening's highlights.

The sweet perfume of night-scented jessamine permeated the air, stealing into Kirsten's soul and making her think things she shouldn't think—things about romance and love and relationships that grew and developed and strengthened with time.

As if attuned to her thoughts, Grant put his arm around her shoulders and drew her close.

'It's a night for love, isn't it?' he murmured. 'Only we've both had the bad luck to fall for the wrong person.'

Kirsten rested her head against his shoulder, accepting the comfort and understanding he was offering.

'I can't keep the ring,' she murmured, wishing with all her heart things could have been different—that this man could have been the one.

CHAPTER EIGHT

THE mood on the ward the following week was sombre. Jack's treatment was so debilitating it seemed that whatever strength had been left in his disease-ravaged body was now being drained away.

With the rooms the unit would eventually use still under modification, Kirsten did what she could, finding big pictures of trucks, tractors and diggers to tape on the glass observation panel in the wall of the isolation room, leaving enough room for people to peer through but filling in most of the big area. She changed these several times a day, so at least, when he turned his head that way, Jack would have something different to look at.

Then, because the other children seemed affected by the atmosphere, she gathered up those not confined to their beds by treatment regimens and started a story game, where they all vied with each other to make the continuing story more and more ridiculous.

'If nothing else, being in hospital expands their imaginations,' one of the parents remarked, as she joined the group.

'We should write down this story,' Alistair suggested. He was a thirteen-year-old who was receiving treatment after having a tumour removed from his abdomen, and at an age when he was fretful over this delay into adolescence.

'Good idea,' Kirsten told him. 'I've got a small recorder, but we'll have to start again tomorrow. Then every night I'll type what we've made up into the computer.'

116

She looked around the group.

'Maybe we can find some pictures to illustrate it and make it into our own book.'

The younger children, who'd been contributing the more bizarre suggestions, decided they'd rather look for pictures while a couple of older ones thought they'd try the drawing and painting programmes on the computer to see if they could do the illustrations they'd need.

The group broke up, and Kirsten began her visits to the other children, checking on the little things that came within her work area. Because weakness limited a patient's range of movement, it was important to check what they could and couldn't reach from the bed when they were hooked up to drips and not well enough to move about with a mobile drip stand. And to provide toys that promoted some muscle movement as well as a bit of diversion.

Squeezy rubber balls, some with strands of rubber hair and others with faces that could be contorted into truly awful expressions, were good for these children, while puzzles could help fill the empty hours.

A little before twelve, she went through to the cloakroom, where she shed the bright T-shirt she'd been wearing, changing into a softly tailored blouse, then adding a jacket, transforming her casual hospital wear into 'smart businesslike' and giving her confidence to tackle the first two of her possible donors.

'Lunch date?'

Of course, she would run into Josh, even though he'd been so busy lately she hadn't had time to tell him she'd finally made Grant accept the ring—and the fact that the engagement was over. And as she hadn't ever worn the ring while working on the children's ward, he was probably assuming she was still engaged.

'With the lucky fiancé no doubt?' he said, his voice as close to a sneer as she'd ever heard.

Ah, well, her assumption had proved correct!

'Not that it's any of your business but, no, it's not Grant—he's gone back to the property. As it happens, this is work-related.'

Kirsten whirled away and Josh, who could have bitten out his tongue for letting some of his pent-up emotion erupt into unrehearsed conversation, turned to watch the way her legs were enhanced by the ridiculously high-heeled sandals she habitually wore, and the way that same footwear made her body move with a swaying motion he found totally mesmerising.

Forget mesmerising and think!

As far as he could make out, Kirsten was still engaged, so the idea of a brief 'getting it out of the way' fling for the two of them was becoming more and more remote, an idea that made various parts of his body ache with frustration.

On the other hand, he was becoming less and less certain that the fling would get it out of the way. Working with her again, he was beginning to realise that the more he saw of her, the more he wanted to see—figuratively as well as literally.

The marriage option sneaked under his mental guard and he did the sums again in his head, but it always came out the same way. Especially not as the new unit needed so much time he couldn't see himself being able to cut back on full-time work and its attendant pressures and commitments for at least another ten years, by which time Kirsten would be thirty-eight. And no matter that women were having babies later, it wasn't quite as easy as the magazine stories made it sound. There were more difficulties with conception, more risk carrying the baby to term and producing a healthy infant.

He couldn't put her through that, even if she was willing to hang around until he reached what he'd figured out was the optimal age for him, as a Phillips male with all the inherent marital problems that entailed, to marry.

Then there was the other problem—the installation of Kirsten's image in place of the cool, calm, competent, controlled 'wife' of his imagination. The mere thought made him shudder. Kirsten was competent enough, but those other 'c' words definitely didn't fit. No, Kirsten was more 'v' words than 'c' words—vibrant, vivid, volatile—

'Are you standing there clutching your sandwich and wondering if you'll be welcome in our tearoom?'

Betty's voice made him start, and he mumbled something, turned about and took his sandwich to his office just outside the ward. He plunked it down on his desk then strode to the window, peering out, though not—definitely not—to check if Kirsten might be walking across the staff car park which was all he overlooked.

He made himself a cup of coffee and sat at his desk. He'd intended eating there in the first place, and catching up on some paperwork at the same time, but he'd seen Kirsten on the ward as he'd walked in and on the faint chance she might be eating there had headed for the tearoom instead.

Only to find she was flitting out to lunch, undoubtedly with some admirer he didn't yet know about.

The surge of totally unexpected jealousy had been the first inkling that she might have become more to him than someone with whom to have a quick and doubtless enjoyable affair.

Damn, but his father was right about not messing with redheads. They got under your skin.

Or this one did, anyway!

He blocked all thoughts of Kirsten out of his head and concentrated on work.

Paperwork!

Facts and figures to be entered on forms, which would doubtless never mean anything to anyone but were still required by the figure-hungry mob in Administration.

Frustrated in more ways than one, he pushed the paperwork aside, choosing instead to go over the procedure he and the oncologist had drawn up for Jack Webster. The little boy had received the chemotherapy drug cyclophosphamide on two successive days and was now undergoing instalments of deep X-ray treatment which would go on for three days. Pathology tests would then, hopefully, prove that all blast cells, the immature cells carrying the programming for the cancer, had been removed.

Someone tapped on the door, then it opened, and Neville Warren, the oncologist who was working with Josh on the problem, came in. He was looking as worried as Josh felt, and in that moment Josh realised he'd been seeking Kirsten's company—thinking about her so much—in an effort to distract himself from the enormity of what they were doing.

'What do you think?' Neville asked, dropping into a chair and slinging his similarly wrapped sandwich onto the desk beside Josh's, then standing up again and heading for Josh's small urn to get himself a cup of coffee.

'I think we're doing the right thing,' Josh said firmly. 'We've the best possible match for Jack with the marrow from his sister, and we need to totally eliminate all traces of the disease. Total body irradiation is the most effective way.'

Neville nodded, took a sip of coffee, then offered Josh a wry smile.

'I guess it's because he's so young I'm worrying,' he admitted. 'With infants we wouldn't have considered the TBI because of the effect of the irradiation on the rest of the body, in particular the brain.'

He was saying things they both knew, but Josh sensed he needed to hear the words to sort out his thoughts. Neville's next words confirmed this.

'But if we'd gone the alternate route, given a second drug like busulphan, we could have missed some of the cells and the whole point of the exercise could have been lost.'

He looked across at Josh.

'How are you feeling about it all?'

'Terrified,' Josh admitted, 'but excited at the same time. I know we're theoretically killing the patient in order to bring him back to life, but there's a far better understanding of the problems associated with bone-marrow transplants now, which means we're better prepared than anyone was in the past. Surely that's a precursor to success.'

Neville nodded, but Josh knew he hadn't lessened Neville's anxiety one bit—any more than similar pep talks he'd been giving to himself had lowered his own tension.

They talked through the alternatives to the decisions they'd made, discussed trials under way in other parts of the country and the world, threw ideas at each other about what might work for future patients. And slowly, for Josh at least, the tension eased.

He unwrapped his sandwich, peered at the filling and realised he'd unwrapped Neville's by mistake. He pushed it across the desk.

'Eat! This is only the beginning. We've weeks of worry ahead of us after the transplant so we'll need all the stamina we can muster. And just think, if we feel this bad, how's the Webster family doing? They understand enough of what's going on to be far more fearful and uncertain than we are.'

Neville looked up.

'I don't know that that's possible,' he told Josh. 'I've worked for ten years in the oncology department here, specialising in children's cancer, but I've never felt this kind of stress. It's as if all my children are lined up in Theatre for heart transplants.'

Josh studied his colleague. They'd come together from different paths, Neville specialising in cancer treatment then sub-specialising in the chemical treatment of children with cancer, while he'd started out as a paediatrician, gravitating to the cancer ward as these patients became more special to him.

For the first time he realised where this difference in training set them apart.

'During paediatrics training we do a reasonable amount of stuff on handling the deaths of children we've been treating. It takes such a toll on a person's emotional health that statistics suggest fifteen years is the absolute maximum anyone should work directly and solely in the area of childhood cancer.'

Neville looked surprised, then he smiled.

'I'm not quite at rock bottom,' he assured Josh, 'but you're right. I might go and talk to someone about this. We tell the parents to share their burdens, to seek help from staff and social workers, but we tend to think we're ten feet tall and bullet-proof.'

'A very dangerous assumption,' Josh told him, then he looked up as another tap on his door heralded a new visitor, one who waited for him to call, 'Come in.'

Kirsten's smile was so radiant his heart jolted in his chest, but she was sharing it equally with Neville so it obviously wasn't personal.

'Guess what?' she demanded, moving into the room and propping herself against the desk so she could include Neville in her news. 'I've got all the equipment we need for the video system and a promise of maintenance on it for life. Of course, being a technology firm, the donors could easily go out of business before the life thing happens, but I'm sure we'd get someone else then, or maybe our own techs could handle it.'

She spread her arms wide and this time the smile was just for Josh.

'Isn't it fabulous? Do you want to tell our maintenance lot or will I? Here's the card of the man to speak to at the video place. It's best if Maintenance talk to him direct so they know what'll be required in the set-up.'

She paused, then perhaps realising Neville had no idea of what she was talking about, smiled just at him and began to explain.

Which gave Josh time to study her and wonder why this particular woman should be affecting him the way she was—the way no other woman had ever affected him.

And right at a time when the last thing he needed was for his personal life to be thrown into turmoil.

So he had to get over it. He had to put her right out of his mind—or at least educate his mind to the fact that she was a colleague and nothing more. He was an intelligent man—he could do that.

She finished explaining her ideas to Neville then turned back to smile at Josh, which was when he realised that educating his mind was one thing—training his body to accept her as a colleague and nothing else was on a par with building a space shuttle in his back yard. That easy!

Then, perhaps sensing the strategy he was attempting to put, at that very moment, into place, she stood up.

'Well, I've taken too much of your time. I just wanted

to let you know, Josh. You'll talk to whoever you need to?'

Without waiting for an answer, she left the room, fortunately closing the door behind her so he was spared a view of her legs disappearing down the corridor.

Kirsten walked away, telling herself it wasn't an escape but simply that she had so much to do now she had the promise of the equipment. She had to get hold of Matt and organise the photos she wanted scanned in for Jack, who'd be shifted into the first of the new rooms the moment it was completed.

She needed to ask Matt about the colour pattern he'd worked out for the walls around the part they'd leave blank for a video screen.

All in all, she had enough to do to keep her mind firmly off Josh Phillips and his maritally dysfunctional family.

The problem was, now she was actually unengaged, Josh seemed to have lost interest, which was understandable, given what was happening in his working life. But where did that leave her?

Available but unwanted—that's where!

Damn it all, was love all about timing after all?

Was there nothing more to it than coincidence of opportunity and availability?

She brought up the subject when she, Alana and Gabi had gathered in Mickey's bar to celebrate the fact they were all off duty together, and to cheer Gabi up, because Alex was away at a conference.

'Now, tell us about the unengagement,' Alana said. 'Is Grant OK with it?'

'Grant took a little time to accept it, but I don't think his heart was broken. He's just ready to settle down, and I happened to be there. At least he's got a ring now for the next woman who pops into his life.'

'Surely he couldn't use the same ring?' Gabi sounded horrified by the thought.

'Why not?' Alana, always the practical one, asked, then she turned again to Kirsten. 'And you? Are you happy about it?'

'Why wouldn't I be? It was my idea.' Kirsten lifted her frosted glass of light beer. 'Here's to singledom!'

Alana lifted her drink in response and they clinked glasses, but she was still studying Kirsten as if not entirely satisfied with her response.

Gabi peered into mineral water she was drinking, smiling secretly to herself—something, Kirsten realised, Gabi was doing more and more often these days.

'Is this smiling at drinks and doors and trees a pregnancy thing?' she asked, then was alarmed when the word 'pregnancy' caused a quivery sensation in her stomach.

Gabi's smile broadened.

'I guess it must be. I didn't realise I was doing it until Alex said something the other day.'

'My guinea pig, Biddy, is pregnant and she doesn't smile,' Alana told her.

'Your guinea pig is always pregnant,' Kirsten reminded her. 'She probably weeps into her pillow, or her wood shavings or whatever, every night.'

'She produces beautiful babies which Darren's pet shop is always able to sell.' Alana spoke in the frosty tones usually reserved for mothers defending the beauty, talent or intelligence of their human offspring.

'Darren takes those babies off your hands because he's in love with you,' Gabi pointed out, and when Alana protested, the other two chuckled, because the aging, myopic Darren was Alana's most devoted admirer, though his love offerings of sick snakes, mutated fish and inbred rats were a trifle strange to say the least.

'Is not!' Alana countered. 'He just knows I'll always give his unsaleable pets a home, and take care of those who've been ill-treated by careless or downright cruel owners.'

Unwilling to get Alana started on animal cruelty and what she'd recommend as punishment—children strung up by their thumbs had once been mentioned—Gabi changed the subject.

'So, who's doing what this weekend? Amuse a pregnant married lady with tales of what attractive singles will be getting up to. Any parties? Blind dates? Un-blind dates? No, that sounds crazy—seeing dates perhaps?'

'I'm going to a symphony concert tomorrow night,' Alana replied. 'Alone, unless I take Biddy in my pocket. Music's supposed to be good for pregnant women. I'm sure it'd be just as good for guinea pigs.'

Gabi looked startled, and as she had known Alana practically all her life, Kirsten was forced to wonder if Alana would actually do such a thing.

'No! Maybe not.' Alana answered her doubts. 'As sure as I did it, I'd get someone huge in the seat next to me and Biddy would be so squashed she'd probably go into labour.'

'So no one's taken the seat on a permanent basis?' Gabi asked, and Alana shook her head.

'Not so far,' she said, 'though I live in hope that eventually some gorgeous music-loving man will shift to town, buy the last remaining months of the season and be given that seat. Then, slowly but surely, the attraction will grow.'

The others laughed at the fantasy, but it triggered something in Kirsten, so when they'd stopped laughing, had ordered their meal and a bottle of wine for her and Alana to share, she returned to the subject.

'Do you think that's how love should happen?' she asked. 'A slow awakening kind of thing? Like getting warm when you've been really, really cold but doing it slowly rather than plunging into a hot bath?'

'Well, I've never heard love described as plunging into a hot bath before,' Alana told her, 'but I can see your point. The physical reaction isn't all that different—your skin feels hot, your pulse throbs, your extremities tingle—'

'If you're really cold and hop into a hot bath, the tingling extremities is chilblains, not love,' Gabi said, and was booed for losing all the romance in her soul now she was happily remarried.

'Not!' she said firmly. 'In fact, being married again, being with Alex, being pregnant—though as you both realise that came before the being married again part—I realise how full of romance my life is. It's like a gigantic romantic dream all come true, so there!'

Once again, Kirsten felt an uneasiness in her stomach, surely not some instinctive nesting thing—not just a quiet ticking, but more a loud *boing* of a biological clock.

Oh, please! That is *so* trite, she told herself, then Alana recalled her to the conversation with a teasing, 'Maybe she's regretting her decision about Grant, and plotting how to get him back again.'

It was a light-hearted comment, but it struck deep into Kirsten's already disturbed emotions.

'I can't quite understand what happened with Grant—I mean, I didn't fall in love with him though maybe I thought I was. Though I don't know that I thought I did, really—it was just that he surprised me with the ring, and suddenly it all seemed possible. You know, being engaged, getting married, white-dress stuff, and what kind of flowers to carry...'

Gabi eyed her with surprise.

'You really are in a muddle, aren't you? First Grant, then the shift back to one of the most stressful jobs in the hospital. It seems to me, for someone who's always had her priorities well worked out—job, clothes, food, men, a really sensible order—you've lost the plot. Though I was pleased to hear the bit about the white dress. At least you've retained something of the Kirsten we both know and love.'

'The clothes mania!' Kirsten said gloomily. 'That's great, isn't it! What's happened to Kirsten? Who knows, but at least she's retained her dress sense!'

Mickey appeared to suggest they shift to a table as their meals were ready, and, still grumbling, Kirsten led the way.

'This is supposed to be a "cheer up Gabi" party,' Gabi reminded her, but Alana touched her arm as if to quieten her.

When they were all seated and their meals had been delivered, Alana filled Kirsten's glass with wine, then said, 'OK, what's really wrong with you, Kirsten? Or should we guess? Two words, starting with JP?'

Kirsten looked at the two women who'd become so close to her. She saw more of Gabi because they lived on the same floor, but in the fifteen months she'd lived in the building she'd come to rely on Alana's common sense and practicality when her own more volatile emotions threatened to overcome her.

'No, it's not Josh.'

She eyed her friends, wondering if she should mention that she'd more or less committed herself to a 'get him out of the system' type fling with him. And that right now she was still seriously considering it, but not sure when, where or how to go about it.

Probably best to not mention it. Gabi would be horrified. Besides, it was going to be such a short-term affair, there was a chance she could get away with them not knowing at all.

But maybe they *could* help with her other problem. The boinging one.

She prodded her fork into a prawn sitting atop her seafood pizza and with a sigh continued her confession.

'You see, I've got this achy kind of feeling in my stomach—a real physical disturbance if you can believe that—and I'm sure it's to do with wanting more than I've got, which, when you think about it, is everything I should want. I mean, I've got a job I love, two degrees, a career I can adapt so I have plenty of variety, and all of a sudden I'm going mushy over wedding dresses, over Gabi being pregnant—and, most terrifying of all, saying yes to the first man who asks me to marry him.'

She took her fork out of the prawn and speared a piece of calamari instead, then added, 'Even if I did say no later.'

'For someone with two degrees, one of which is psychology, you don't have many insights into your own problem,' Alana said.

She winked at Gabi, who was tucking into her vegetarian lasagne with obvious enjoyment.

'Which is?' Kirsten demanded, cross because they were both amused at her expense but, in her heart of hearts, not really blaming them. She'd be amused herself if it hadn't been her in this predicament.

'Nesting syndrome.'

Alana echoed her own instinctive thought when she'd heard the 'boing' earlier.

'Damn! Do you think it could be? Do you think such a thing exists?'

'Not in psychological literature obviously,' Gabi teased. 'But out of the textbooks and into real life—I think it does. Hell, you're the one who's always doing the quizzes—haven't you done the ones that ask, "Are you ready to marry and settle down? Score each answer one with a four, answer two with a three", etcetera.'

Kirsten ate the calamari, pondering as she chewed.

'You know, I don't think I have,' she admitted. 'I usually do the ones about "Finding Mr Right" and "Who'll be your perfect match?" or "Is your man ready for commitment?".'

'And does Josh Phillips ever meet any of their criteria?'

Kirsten sighed—she seemed to be sighing all the time these days.

'He comes out as Mr Wrong every time,' she admitted sadly, still playing with her food while the other two tackled theirs with gusto. 'While as far as the commitment ones go, he wouldn't even score, so I don't bother trying those where he's concerned.'

'We're wandering off track,' Alana said. 'Which is your internal problems. If your body thinks it's time to start getting serious about becoming one of a couple, then mother of a burgeoning family, I'd say you should go with it. Bodies often know what's best for us, and we don't listen to them nearly enough.'

'This from a woman who's dating a pregnant guinea pig,' Kirsten scoffed, but only because Alana's words had been even more unsettling than the clock business earlier.

'But how?'

Gabi asked the question Kirsten should have asked.

'I mean,' Gabi continued, 'how do you go about it? With me and Alex, it just happened—we were sitting beside each other in one of the first lectures we had at uni, and it went from there. But in Kirsten's case, she's just knocked back one, even if I do say so myself, perfectly good offer of marriage, and the man she'd really like to marry—or thinks she'd like to marry—is off-limits for reasons we all know too well, so where does that leave her? Hanging around singles' bars? We've all done that from time to time over the past year when I was single with you, and we always ended up coming home together, pulling the men we *had* met to pieces on the way.'

'Only because they were usually all losers,' Kirsten reminded her. 'Remember the one who told Alana he had his pet ferret down his trousers and wanted to show it to her?'

'You attracted your share of weird types, but I won't dignify this conversation by mentioning them.' Alana glared at her, then brightened perceptibly. 'What about the internet?' she asked. 'Rarely a day goes by without one of us hearing a story about someone who's met her perfect match on the net.'

'And one or other of the so-called perfect couple is usually married to someone else at the time,' Kirsten said gloomily. 'It's like a disease. Where's the sanctity of marriage? Worse, why am I even contemplating it?'

'Consider it as purely anti-emetic,' Alana said in a kindly tone. 'To stop the problem with your stomach. Now, how do we find out what's the best internet dating service?'

'*We* find out?' Kirsten echoed faintly. This was getting out of hand, and she really didn't want to find anyone right now. Not when she had the 'fling' to attend to first.

Maybe after that she'd be able to consider other men...

'Of course *we*,' Alana responded. 'Do you think we're going to let you have all the fun?' She grinned at Kirsten. 'Besides,' she added, 'if it works for you I might try it myself.'

They finished their meal, and while Gabi excused herself because she was expecting a call from Alex, Kirsten and Alana headed for Kirsten's flat where Alana, bulldozing over Kirsten's protests, started a search for dating agencies.

'Profile. We need a profile of you.'

Alana, reading from the screen, pointed out this necessity.

'That's easy. Height, weight, colouring and profession—that's enough, isn't it?'

'No way. You've got to make yourself sound fantastic—really interesting. I'll do it.'

So while Alana worked the old-fashioned way, with pen and paper, to construct the perfect profile for Kirsten—'luscious curvaceous redhead, fond of games' was deleted as fast as it was offered—Kirsten checked her emails.

'So, who's Matt? And why are we looking for a man for you if you already have a Matt asking you to dinner?'

Alana, obviously bored with the profile, was now reading over Kirsten's shoulder.

'It's work,' Kirsten said. 'He wants to talk about a computer program he's setting up for the isolation rooms on the ward.'

'So?' Alana demanded. 'He's a man, isn't he? If you're getting Josh out of your life, you have to start somewhere.'

'He's Josh's cousin so that won't wash.'

Alana's eyes lit up.

'Won't wash! Girl, it's ideal. This might come with illuminating brilliance to you, but you're not actually over Josh. And, roll of drums, newsflash, you might never be! You're not the slightest bit interested in finding someone else—look who's working on your profile here! No, Josh is the man for you, and though, for whatever feeble reason, he's not playing, you can't say the man's not interested.'

She paused for breath, which was when Kirsten should probably have told her about the fling, but before she'd plucked up the courage, Alana continued.

'So, what we need is a plan. It's a good thing Gabi isn't here, as she has more conscience than you and I, so she might have felt obliged to make the odd petty objection. But going out with his cousin is a very good start. Is he good-looking, the cousin? If so, perhaps you could ask him to bring his cousin Josh as a blind date for your friend—me—and then I could take Matt off your hands and you'd end up with Josh.'

'But you'd only take Matt off my hands if he's good-looking?' Kirsten shook her head. 'You call that friendship? A plan?'

'I'm just thinking out loud,' Alana said, trying for offended dignity but missing by a mile. 'But going out with his cousin still has possibilities. I don't suppose you'd consider throwing yourself in front of his car?'

'Stop!' Kirsten held up her hand. 'Now, start over. How is my going out with Matt going to help anything? While as for throwing myself in front of his car, I don't even know what he drives, and having two broken legs and probably head injuries isn't exactly what we're aiming for here.'

'I don't mean Matt's car, you goose. I'm talking about Josh's wonderful machine—and you wouldn't have to throw yourself right into its path, maybe just let it bump you. He'd rush to pick you up, hold you in his arms, and—nearly losing you—would realise how much he loves you.'

Alana started making kissy, smoochy noises, and

Kirsten found herself grinding her teeth with the frustration of not biting one of her best friends.

With that option ruled out—after all, she hadn't really bitten anyone since kindergarten and then had been smacked quite hard—she had to content herself with a firm 'No'.

This was obviously the time to tell Alana that the 'holding in his arms' bit was already organised—it would be an essential part of the fling—but that the love realisation wasn't part of the arrangement.

Only she wasn't sure enough about anything to mention it just yet, and anyway Alana was talking again…

'It was only an idea, but I'll admit not one of my best. But as nothing else seems to be on offer, we'll have to stick with Matt,' she said. 'Going out with him is a good start to your new life. Answer the email—ask him where and when.'

Kirsten hesitated, not at all happy about the thought of an evening alone with Matt. But they did need to discuss the program—and maybe she could talk to him about computer programming in general and find out what courses would be available—something new to learn…

'Now!' Alana ordered. 'Answer him now, and pray he's online so he can e-mail back straight away with the name of a restaurant.'

'Why does that matter?' Kirsten asked, as she typed in a reply and sent it winging through cyberspace. She was confused but not overly suspicious about the level of Alana's interest.

Which was a good thing, because all she got by way of an answer was a look of disbelief.

'Surely you know why.' Alana shook her head in shock at such ignorance. 'There's a world of meaning in choice of restaurants. La Fenice is so upmarket and intimate it's proposal stuff, so I doubt he'd take you there for a first date.'

She ignored Kirsten's interjection of, 'It's not a date.'

'Rusillo's is good. It's a "let's eat together and see if we might get on—if we laugh at the same things, find common ground" kind of place. But it's expensive so it's one up on Mickey's where you could do the same thing but not as seriously. The Blue Room—well, even you must know it's the ultimate seduction venue. Piano bar, moody music, dim lights gleaming off white damask and silver candlesticks, selectively placed greenery to ensure each table's privacy. I've often wondered why they don't have rooms available upstairs so guests who get too hot for each other could repair there rather than go all the way home.'

'Y-you've got to be j-joking!' Kirsten stuttered. 'This can't be true. I went to The Blue Room with my psych mentor!'

Alana smiled indulgently.

'The one who spent the entire year trying to get you into his bed?'

Oh!

'How do you know all this?' Rather than admit that Alana *might* have a point as far as that particular male was concerned, Kirsten went on the attack.

Alana grinned at her.

'I did have a social life once upon a time,' she said. 'I've been to all of them and eventually one of the hope-fuls, realising we'd make better friends than lovers, explained it to me. It's like a code—comes out in the guys' handbook, or maybe they write it up on the wall in those last bastions of the male—football locker rooms.'

'So what happened to it?'

'To football locker rooms? Writing on the walls?' Alana looked as perplexed as she sounded.

'To your social life?' Kirsten said, when that part of Alana's conversation struck her as odder than all the rest. 'You said you did have one once.'

Alana smiled, then chuckled in the sexy way she had which had often made Kirsten wonder why she didn't have a man in her life.

'I got tired of it all. None of them clicked, nothing happened. No lights flashing, no pulses racing, no stomach upheavals—nothing. And in the end I decided it was all taking up too much time. I made a conscious decision to stop looking and get on with the rest of my life, do the things *I* wanted to do. I love going to clubs but that's for the dancing, not a manhunt, and I go to the theatre because I love that too, and it totally relaxes me. I've got my animals, I love my job, and if a man happens to turn up in my life, well, that's OK, but if not, then that's OK as well.'

Kirsten absorbed all this, amazed she was still finding out things about Alana, then she grinned.

'If one happens to turn up?' she repeated. 'I don't suppose the person who bought the season ticket next to you at the theatre then handed it back in, once subscriptions had closed, was one Alana Wright?'

'As if I would!' Alana retorted, but Kirsten still wondered. There were times when the highly practical and organised and together Alana showed very romantic tendencies!

But before she could push further, Alana was all business again.

'Come on, check your emails again. See if Matt's replied.'

He had.

Great. I'll see if I can get a table at The Blue Room tomorrow. I heard it had been booked out for a wedding party, but that's been called off so we should be right. I'll pick you up at seven-thirty if that's all right with you.

Kirsten stared at the message in dismay.

'I can't go to The Blue Room with Matt now you've told me what it means,' she wailed.

'Of course you can,' Alana told her. 'You'd have gone if I hadn't told you, and if he's the kind of man you say he is, you'd have trouble with him coming on too strong wherever you go. So go for the food—which you must admit is heavenly. Have a piece of the chocolate macadamia torte for me.'

Alana's confidence and enthusiasm were so strong Kirsten found herself weakly replying to the message, assuring Matt she'd be ready for him at seven-thirty.

'You could have asked him to come earlier and have a drink,' Alana told her, but Kirsten shook her head. Going out with Matt was purely business, but it was also good practice for going out with other men after she'd finished the fling—should they ever find time for it.

Alana's motivation for pushing her into this date was obviously to make Josh jealous, but that wouldn't work because the man didn't care about her anyway.

Not beyond the physical attraction which would be taken care of before too long, anyway.

Neither would he know about the date, so how could he possibly be jealous?

CHAPTER NINE

WAKING early next morning, Kirsten's first thoughts were for little Jack Webster. How was he doing? How would the irradiation have affected him? How were his parents coping?

Realising it would occupy her mind until she knew, she got up, showered, pulled on a pair of cut-off jeans and a T-shirt with a vivid parrot splashed across the front and headed for the hospital.

Once outside, the lack of traffic on the streets, the un-earthly kind of quiet, made her check the time.

'Six o'clock! You're up at six o'clock on a Saturday morning?'

Her cries of disbelief echoed back to her, while the horror of it had her gasping, but little Jack had been with her in her dreams and she had to see him. She walked on towards the hospital but stopped at a small café half a block away. It was always open early to catch night staff coming off duty.

One or other of Jack's parents had probably been up all night with him, and though they would have been offered hospital tea, coffee and snacks, the institutional food was generally unappealing.

She'd take them a treat.

Inside the café, the smell of freshly ground beans mingled with the delicious smell of baking—sugary baking. Kirsten ordered three coffees—a cappuccino, latte and one black. She could take her coffee any way, and this way she could offer the Websters a choice. While this was being prepared she surveyed the delicacies on offer, settling eventually on a mix of croissants, doughnuts, friands and muffins.

With it all packed in an open box, she set off again, entering the hospital through the main entrance which had automatic doors and so was easier for someone balancing three coffees and food.

Up on the sixth floor she stopped briefly to ask a nurse going off duty if she knew how Jack was doing, but the woman had been in 6B, the children's orthopaedic ward, and hadn't heard.

Kirsten proceeded on her way, setting her box down on the desk at the nurses' station and smacking at the grasping hands reaching out for her goodies.

'They're for the Websters,' she said firmly. 'I thought they'd probably had a rough night.'

All the nurses nodded, and most went back to the jobs they'd been doing when Kirsten had walked in. Annie, the staff nurse in charge, remained and she nodded soberly.

'But there's so much worse to come, not so much in terms of him being sicker but certainly in terms of time. He's going to be sick like this for weeks.'

Kirsten nodded.

'Now's bad because although he'd been sick before during the treatment, they probably didn't realise just how much worse he'd get with the higher dosage of drugs and radiation. Once they get used to it, it might get easier.'

Annie didn't look convinced.

'I just find it hard to handle the fact that we have to make him *so* sick. I mean, we're doing it deliberately.'

'But only in an attempt to ultimately save his life,' Kirsten reminded her. She might have sounded hopeful but Annie's concern had left a hard, cold lump in her chest. Fortunately, before she could get too upset, she remembered the coffee, and with the excuse that it would get cold she lifted her box and moved across the ward, winking at children who were awake and finally coming to the room where Jack was isolated.

She set down her box on a small table outside the room, then peered through the glass, her heart apparently recognising Josh a split second before her eyes if the rapid acceleration of beats was any indication.

He was talking to Mrs Webster but, perhaps sensing Kirsten's presence, he glanced up, saw her and frowned.

Great! Had she broken some rule she didn't know about, coming in to see a patient on a Saturday?

Still frowning, he said something to Mrs Webster who turned and waved, then, as Kirsten held up a polystyrene coffee cup, the woman beamed and started towards the door, stripping off the gown and mask she was wearing and leaving them on a hook inside the door.

'Real coffee? For me? Bless you, Kirsten!' Then she saw the array of sweet treats in the box, and her delight grew even more apparent.

'You darling!' she said, giving Kirsten a one-armed hug and falling on a doughnut with great enthusiasm.

'I brought enough for your husband—he's not here?'

Mrs Webster shook her head.

'Although we've got fantastic friends and family to help out, one of us likes to be with the other kids, especially with Linda who knows she has to come to hospital soon but doesn't fully understand about the bone-marrow harvest. I put them to bed last night and slept until about one, then came up here and he went home. He'll do the getting-up things and come back later to relieve me.'

She'd chosen the latte and was sugaring it when Josh came out of the room.

He looked terrible—as if he'd had even less sleep than Mrs Webster.

'Coffee? I've black or cappuccino,' Kirsten told him. 'And cake for a quick carbohydrate boost.'

'I thought bananas were the best quick carbohydrate boost,' he said, declaring combat with his first utterance.

'But so boring,' Kirsten countered. 'Go on, be a devil, have a cake.'

He took the black coffee, sugared it, then carefully studied the selection. Mrs Webster stole a chocolate doughnut from under his hovering fingers.

'Too slow,' she told him, peering through the glass to make sure Jack was still sleeping.

'How is he?' Kirsten asked, as Josh weakened and picked up a still warm blueberry muffin.

'Not good,' Mrs Webster said. 'If I'd known how sick he'd be…' She glanced apologetically at Josh. 'I know you told me, but it doesn't always sink in. And I know he has to be this sick if you're to have any chance at all of curing him, but the poor darling is nauseated and vomiting and in obvious pain. Josh is doing what he can to control it, but it's still terrible.'

It sounded terrible, so much so that Kirsten turned anxiously to Josh.

'He hasn't picked up an infection already, has he?'

He shook his head but didn't speak, and while that might have had something to do with a mouthful of blueberry muffin, the look in his eyes suggested otherwise.

Suggested he didn't want to speak—at least not to her.

And if he did speak, the look also conveyed that it wouldn't be to say thanks for the coffee, or anything else either pleasant or polite. Oh, no, the look was so severe she actually checked her body to make sure she was wearing clothes—after all, at this hour who could be sure?

Then she tried to remember if there was another rule about staff not wearing parrot-emblazoned T-shirts in the hospital even if they were off duty.

Mrs Webster was talking, explaining the various symptoms the little boy was showing as a result of his treatment. 'But worst of all is the boredom. He's too sick to sleep a lot of the time, and when he's awake he's not sure what he wants. I tell him stories and we've been changing the pictures outside his window, and he's allowed some toys which have been treated before coming into the room, but I think it's because he's so sick he's easily distracted, so he's easily bored.'

'We'll have him in one of the new rooms soon,' Josh promised her. 'And if everything works out as we hope it will, he'll have things to do and see.'

He turned to Kirsten and said, with ultra-cool reserve, 'Have you seen the walls? The painters have incorporated Matt's design, but I guess you knew that.'

Kirsten bit back an urge to snap, 'No, I didn't.' Mainly because it might upset Mrs Webster. Besides that, the man's mood was so black that arguing with him might provoke violence.

She finished her coffee, explaining at the same time the theory behind painting the walls.

'We're also setting up individual videos for each child so if he's got a favourite book we can scan that in, then show it on part of the wall. I've a heap of pictures of heavy machinery already scanned, and I've emailed them to Josh's cousin Matt, who's programming all of this for us.'

'Isn't that wonderful?' Mrs Webster said. 'He must be a very special man.'

Inside the room, Jack was stirring, so his mother finished her coffee quickly, left the cup on the tray, washed her hands, then headed back into the isolation room, pausing in the doorway to smile fondly at Josh and add, 'You're a very special family.'

Josh at least waited until she was out of earshot before he muttered a grating, and very cynical, 'Tell me about it!'

Not wanting to antagonise him even more, Kirsten finished her coffee and went through to the far end of the ward to see the painted walls. She was squinting at the pattern, trying to work out the different images that could be made from the shapes and colours, when someone else walked in.

The someone else she'd come this way to avoid.

'Is this what you wanted?' he asked, though his tone was verging on demand.

'I think it's great!' she said. 'Even squinting you can see some of the animals and objects. Look, if you stand here and squint, there's a birthday cake, and up in that corner—'

'I'm not talking about the wall.' The words grated down her spine. 'I meant, is this what you wanted as far as you and I are concerned? Passionate kisses, a promise for the future, pleas to get unengaged first—and now? A limbo state, with nothing happening? Is that it?'

When she didn't reply he reached out and lifted her left hand, which suddenly seemed conspicuously bare.

'No fiancé?'

'No fiancé,' she confirmed, the words practically stuttering off her lips—no doubt the result of hand-to-hand contact. 'I've been meaning to talk to you about that.'

She gathered all her reserves of strength and looked into the blueness of his eyes.

'I said I'd go ahead—have an affair with you—and I'm OK with that.' Had it been physically possible, she'd have patted herself on the back for sounding so together. 'But I think we should establish some ground rules first.'

Good, she'd managed to startle him, by the look of things—without fainting or stammering or even going more than slightly pink.

'Ground rules?' The words growled into the air between them.

'Yes,' Kirsten told him, standing straighter as her confidence rose. 'Parameters—that kind of thing. For a start, I'd like to know how long your affairs usually last. Are we talking a month? Six weeks?'

Startled didn't begin to describe his expression now. Stunned came close but didn't quite make it either.

'Is this the same woman who walked out of my bedroom less than twelve months ago because I didn't want to make a long-term commitment? The same woman who talked about bonsai trees and stunted growth, though where the horticultural theme fitted I was never quite sure?'

Heat, which was probably making her cheeks more than slightly pink, rose in Kirsten but she stood her ground.

'That was different. As far as I was concerned, going to bed with you back then would have been the beginning of a relationship that might have had somewhere to go. But now I know your rules, and now we're only doing it to get the lust problem out of our systems, I thought we should put some kind of time limit on it. I'm not up on flings, but *you* must know how long your affairs usually last.'

Josh began to wonder if maybe he was asleep and this was all a very peculiar dream. But though he often dreamt in colour—and there was plenty of colour here—he rarely smelt perfume in his dreams, and there was definitely perfume in this one.

A sultry, smoky kind of perfume that aroused images of deserted cabins in the bush and a russet-haired woman naked by a fire—

He shook his head to clear the image away, checked the redhead had clothes on, winced slightly at the vibrancy of the parrot on said clothes, then battled his way back into her weird conversation.

'I haven't actually, consciously, timed my past affairs,' he said, attempting, with difficulty, to keep the growl out of his voice. Then, the moment the words were out of his mouth, he regretted them. He'd made it sound as if his life was one long string of short associations with temporary lovers, whereas, in truth, he was so involved with his work most of the women who'd passed through his life hadn't been willing to put up with his erratic working hours for longer than a couple of months.

Though he'd never admitted the bit about the women usually leaving him to anyone. He was content to be seen as the proverbial playboy, moving on from one woman to another, because it suited his own plan to avoid commitment until much later in his life.

In that way, Kirsten had been different right from the start. For some unknown reason, and later to his great regret, he'd felt obliged to talk to her about the commitment thing—to be honest about the relationship not having a future.

'So, shall we say four weeks?'

Her voice interrupted these depressing thoughts, but the words didn't make much sense.

'Four weeks for what?'

'For our fling—our affair,' Kirsten said gently, then she leaned forward and kissed him on the lips. 'In Michael's glade, remember? I agreed we should get it out of the way. It's what we started talking about when you came in here just now. The end of the limbo. I'm free from tomorrow morning. No, make that tomorrow afternoon—I might sleep in tomorrow morning.'

Josh closed his eyes and prayed for patience.

It didn't come but he hadn't strangled her yet so that was good.

But how did you handle a woman who was making an appointment to start an affair in much the same way as normal people made an appointment to see their doctor?

Go with the flow, you idiot, part of him said, while another part rebelled at her coldly clinical attitude.

Then she kissed him again—to seal the deal, she whispered—and he thought, To hell with the clinical attitude, I'll go with the flow.

Kissed her back, and when it seemed that any moment they'd be stripping off each other's clothes right there in a partly finished hospital isolation room, he pulled away.

'Why wait until tomorrow? Have dinner with me tonight and you can sleep in, in my bed. I'll even cook you breakfast, or brunch, or whatever seems appropriate.'

He was still holding her so was close enough to see the spark of excitement dim in her eyes, to be replaced by a look that he could only describe as guilty.

'Well…the thing is…ah…it's like this…'

'You can't make tonight?'

Red-brown hair flicked from side to side as she shook her head.

'No. Sorry. I've got a—meeting.'

He didn't believe her—not for one minute. She had a date tonight!

Tonight! The night before she was coolly and calmly planning to begin her affair with him!

Well, to hell with her, Josh thought as he spun away.

There were plenty of available women out there who'd be only too glad to enjoy his company—in and out of bed.

But before he reached the door, parts of his body reminded him of why those available women had failed to attract him lately, and why, if he didn't get Kirsten Collins out of his system once and for all, they would continue to not attract him.

However, he wouldn't give in yet. He wouldn't let her know he was willing to toe whatever line she happened to draw in the sand. He'd let her sweat.

He checked on Jack one more time, then decided he should get some sleep. A lot of sleep if this weekend was going to prove 'The One'.

CHAPTER TEN

THE tall blonde woman in the lift seemed vaguely familiar, bringing Kirsten to mind.

'Alana Wright,' she said, holding out her hand as she reminded him of her name. 'I live in Near West near Gabi and Alex Graham, and the Frosts and, of course, Kirsten.'

Josh managed to stay close to her as more people got in. If she lived near Kirsten...

He was wondering how to start the conversation—'Do you know much about Kirsten's social life?' seemed a trifle obvious—when she spoke again.

'So, The Blue Room tonight? That should be fun. The food's divine.'

'The Blue Room?' he echoed, totally at sea with this strange conversational twist. He knew the restaurant, of course, but why would Alana bring it up?

'You and Kirsten,' she said, as if his thoughts had prodded her into explaining. 'Oh, don't worry, she doesn't prattle on about her dates, but she was so excited when she told me she was going, I guessed it had to be you.'

The lift doors opened, and Alana stepped out, and before Josh could follow to demand more explanations, the doors slid shut.

'Why is my life so beset with infuriating women?' he demanded, not quite under his breath from the strange looks the other passengers gave him.

He got out of the lift at the next floor, and went back up to six, not wanting to see Kirsten—he *might* just strangle her if he did—but to reach the safety of his office where he hoped to be able to think.

If his brain was still capable of such a basic process.

He phoned his mother.

'Dinner tonight? At The Blue Room? Darling, I haven't been there for years. I'd love it. But don't come all the way out here to pick me up. I'll come to you. Is it OK if I stay the night, or are there more than two of us on this date?'

'No, just us,' he assured her.

Alana, meanwhile, had managed to bump into Kirsten, though it was a wonder someone hadn't called Security, the way she'd been lurking around the corridors and lift foyers up on six. She'd realised the previous evening that Josh Phillips would be bound to do a Saturday morning ward round and, determined to catch him, had been there for what seemed like hours. Catching Kirsten there as well had been a bonus.

'Did you ever buy that slinky black dress we saw at El Centro a few weeks ago?' she asked, hoping clothes-conscious Kirsten would accept this as a reasonably normal remark.

'The one with the deep V-neck? No!' The regret in Kirsten's voice was enough to give Alana hope.

'OK, then if you've nothing else to do, let's go and get it now. I didn't give you anything for Christmas, so I'll put in. And Gabi gave you a voucher that can be spent in any store in the centre, so you can put that towards it as well.'

Kirsten turned to her, frowning now.

'Why do I need a new black dress?' she demanded, then she weakened and added, 'Though it was divine, wasn't it?'

'You could wear it out with Matt tonight,' Kirsten pointed out. 'After all, The Blue Room is very special.'

'But Matt isn't.' Kirsten heaved a deep sigh. 'It's business, not a date.'

'Well, I've never known that make any difference to you. It's not as if it's a formal ball gown, just a drop-dead gorgeous dress that happens to suit you so beautifully it's actually a shame it's still sitting in the shop.'

'It might not be,' Kirsten said, but she knew she was weakening. The dress had looked great on her, and surely she and Josh wouldn't spend the entire four weeks in bed. Or had they settled on six weeks? Surely they'd go out to eat occasionally…

'OK,' she said, thinking of the way Josh's eyes would gleam when he saw her in it.

'Great! Then, if you're finished here, let's go!' Alana said, which was when Kirsten wondered what Alana was doing at the hospital that morning.

And fast on the heels of that thought came the realisation that Alana would also expect to see her in the dress tonight!

Oh, well, what the heck. And at least if she felt great, it would help her get through the evening with Matt. As long as he didn't think she was dressing specially for him…

'Why is life so complicated?' she moaned, following Alana out of the building.

But complicated didn't begin to cover the mess that developed later. First of all, a low-cut dress was not the kind of thing to encourage Matt to keep his hands to himself, and when he wasn't touching her he was ogling her chest where, considering the depth of the V, it was perfectly obvious she wasn't wearing a bra.

'OK,' she said, when twenty minutes in his company on the drive to the restaurant had convinced her they needed to talk. 'Let's just get a few things straight.'

They'd pulled into the parking area so she had most of his attention, though his eyes kept straying downwards.

'We are out together on business,' she reminded him sternly. 'And, yes, I probably made a mistake wearing this dress, but you're a grown man and surely mature enough to be able to control your baser instincts.'

She tilted his chin up with a forefinger so she could see where he was looking.

'For the duration of this meal, you will sit opposite me, and we will talk about videos and scanning stuff, and machinery and computerised images, and you will not touch me or drop your eyes below my chin. And so you don't feel you're being cheated in any way, I'll pay for dinner.'

He saluted, gave her a smart 'Yes, ma'am' then grinned at her, and for a split second she wondered why she'd ended up so hopelessly hooked on his cousin. Going out with Matt might have been fun.

'But don't imagine you'll always have the last word,' he warned. 'I'm not a man who gives up easily.'

So they were laughing when they walked in, and still relaxed with each other as they were shown to a discreet corner table.

'I asked for it because we'd be working,' Matt said, when she turned and raised her eyebrows at him. He lifted a small case which she hadn't noticed he'd been carrying. 'I've some new ideas to show you.'

She was surprised enough to give him a light kiss on the cheek.

'You are wonderful,' she said. 'I was visiting one of the patients today and he's so fractious. Most of it is because he's so sick, but it's also boredom. I need whatever you can give me to get his mind off feeling so bad.'

They sat down, ordered drinks, then, while Matt started his computer, Kirsten looked around the room—or as much of it as she could see for the protective greenery.

The cancelled wedding reception had left it less crowded than usual but the tables were filling up. Directly opposite her was an older woman who looked vaguely familiar. Perhaps she'd been a patient. Patients always looked different when encountered beyond the hospital walls.

Then someone joined the woman, and though Kirsten's only view was a darkly suited back she recognised the breadth of shoulders, the slant down to a slim waist and hips—and the hair which, at the moment, was still freshly combed so smooth and neat and tidy.

Her heart did a side-step, and her stomach niggled uneasily, but her mind kept insisting that she preferred the hair a little mussed and wondering if she'd have the opportunity to muss it tomorrow. Had they agreed to start? She couldn't remember. It seemed as if every time they'd spoken recently they'd ended up fighting.

Joy Phillips—the familiarity had been explained when Josh had appeared—waved, and Kirsten, certain the woman wouldn't know her out of the Dolly Parton wig, looked around to see if there was someone behind them.

Of course, there wasn't and, anyway, Matt was waving back. One assumed, as she was his aunt, she'd recognised him not Kirsten.

Great! Now Josh had turned and was looking at them, and even at this distance she could see his frown.

'Damn!' Matt said. 'I haven't seen Joy for ages. I'd better go and do the dutiful. Look, I've started this, just use the cursor to follow the program. I've put in written prompts in bubbles, but will add voice prompts for the kids when we get the real thing going.'

He pushed the laptop across to Kirsten, who was so thankful for a diversion she could have kissed him—again!

She studied the picture then followed the prompts, delighted to find how easy the program was to work, and how many diverse pictures it could produce. The bubble in which the prompts were written was attached to a little mechanical man, who performed any manner of antics as he made his suggestions. And when she hesitated, he tapped his foot as if impatient with her.

She was laughing at his antics when she sensed someone approach, and as she was expecting either Matt, or the waiter returning with their drinks, the arrival of Josh startled her.

'A meeting, huh?' he said, sliding into the chair Matt had vacated.

'Yes!' she snapped. 'Do you want to see the computer program we're discussing?'

But Josh couldn't answer, his mouth too dry from the effect of a deep black V in the dress she was almost wearing, which drew his eyes to the slight suggestive swell of beautiful breasts.

And she was out with his cousin? The most licentious member of the family?

'You met my mother the other night at the Bush Dance, so you'd know she's joined the committee. Why don't we all have dinner together? She'd love to see the program and as it's only a *meeting*, I guess Matt wouldn't mind.'

He'd managed to raise his eyes to her face by now, and smiled as he saw the little freckles darken, a sure sign heat was creeping into her cheeks. One up to him. Now he'd push her a little further!

'And while Matt's showing my mother the programs, we can discuss arrangements. Did you have a special time in mind tomorrow? Would you like to come to my place? You could shift in if you like. Or would you like me to come to your place?'

'No!'

The word was so loud it must have shocked her, for she looked guiltily around, then tried a pathetic smile at the waiter bringing drinks.

Josh spoke to him, pointed out his mother and Matt and organised the shift to the table where he and Kirsten were.

As the man walked away, Josh turned his attention back to Kirsten, delighted to see she looked as bewildered as he'd felt this morning when she'd demanded they make ground rules for the 'fling', as she insisted on calling it.

But if he'd expected her to back down, he was wrong. She tilted her chin, and the defiance in the gesture stirred his body almost as much as the shadowy breasts had. She studied him for a moment as if making sure he was serious, then, as Matt and his mother approached the table, she said, 'I couldn't possibly shift in—it'd take all month to pack my clothes—but I'd be happier at your place.'

'Less gossip, too?'

She shrugged. 'There's that.'

Kirsten looked at him and hoped the confusion she was feeling wasn't reflected in her eyes. Looked at him and ached with wanting him, but at the same time feeling that this cold-blooded affair—no, damn it all, that was wrong, it was the hot-bloodedness that was causing all the problems—well, whatever it was—the fling—wasn't right.

It wasn't *her*, and she didn't need a pop psychology quiz to tell her she was going to feel badly about it. Neither did she intend to admit to her friends that she was doing something so insane.

But if it got even a little of the wanting him out of the way...

Josh stood up, pulled out a chair for his mother, and was holding it, reminding her of who Kirsten was, playing host at Matt's table.

Matt!

Kirsten glanced at him and caught the apologetic shrug of his shoulders.

'Family!' he said, as if that explained everything, then, as he sat and edged his chair a little closer to hers, he added, 'Good thing it wasn't a date!'

He then proceeded to show Joy the programs he'd devised, explaining in great detail how they worked. Kirsten watched the way the woman listened, saw the intelligence in her eyes as she grasped the different concepts, then used the touch pad to change images.

But though she watched Joy and Matt, her entire body was aware of Josh on her other side, the little hairs on her arms and legs erect with their knowledge of his presence.

'This was your idea?' Joy said to Kirsten. 'It's brilliant.'

'It's Matt's work,' Kirsten protested, surprised the words came out so clearly because her brain was clogged by desire. 'Ideas are one thing, working out how to turn them into something real—that's way beyond me.'

'Not in every field, I hope,' Josh murmured, and a fiery heat surging through her body added to her physical problems.

A waiter arrived to take their order, and the computer was shut down.

'At least then we can pretend we're out to enjoy a civilised dinner together,' Josh said, though the way Kirsten was feeling, civilised was way off base.

Joy asked about the two special rooms, about how Jack

was doing, and although Josh answered most of her questions, Kirsten was drawn in. Then Joy, perhaps realising Matt was being left out, reminded him of holidays he'd had out at her place.

'You were the only one of all the kids who sat inside and played with the computer while the others rode, or swam in the creek, or generally ran wild.'

'It was the only computer I was ever allowed to use,' Matt reminded her. 'Dad had one at home but it was in his office and that place was sacrosanct. It wasn't until I was in my last years at high school he finally got himself a new one and passed the old one on to me.'

Kirsten heard a roughness in his voice, as if this silly little memory had prompted emotions he didn't want to feel—or remember. She glanced from him to Josh, wondering about the Phillips men and what effect their fathering skills—or lack thereof—had had on their sons.

And while they joked and played 'do you remember' about their childhood holidays, she felt again that tingling, weakening rush of love for Josh that had prompted her to decide a month with him was better than nothing.

What she had to guard against was him realising this was what she felt, because if he ever caught even an inkling of it, she'd be out of his life before she could say the word 'commitment'.

'I'm sorry, I was miles away,' she said to Joy, when she realised the older woman had leant across the table to ask her something.

'I wondered if you're seeing much of Matt. Is something going on between you?'

Kirsten smiled as she shook her head.

'No, we've just been working on this project together. In fact, I'm buying him dinner by way of a thank you.'

Josh must have heard for he turned and his blue eyes

looked hard into hers as if testing the truth of this statement. Then they softened, which brought back a now familiar problem with her knees, and he said softly, 'Actually, I should pay. After all, it's my project, and I
dragged Matt into it.'

'Fine by me,' Matt said, then he grinned evilly at his
cousin. 'But I still get to drive the girl home!'

'He's crazy about you,' Matt said to her, when they
were driving home after they'd enjoyed a wonderful meal,
talked and laughed a lot, and had generally had a good,
if from Kirsten's perspective, slightly uncomfortable evening.

'Rubbish,' she said. 'It's a challenge, nothing more. I'm
probably the last remaining single woman in the hospital
he hasn't slept with.'

'And are you going to change that situation?' he asked,
sliding a glance her way.

'None of your business,' she snapped, and he chortled
with delight.

'That means yes! Oh, dear, you do know what you're
doing, don't you? We're hopeless cases, all the Phillips
men. I thought my father was bad, totally distancing himself from his kids, but at least he kept Mum around. Uncle
Harold didn't even pretend to care, though he must have
gone home to Joy at least three times, unless she cheated
on him, but given the way the boys all turned out—work-
aholics like their father—that's unlikely.'

'I think you use it as an excuse,' Kirsten told him. 'It's
easier to blame your genes than to expend the emotion
required to have a real relationship. Oh, we're Phillipses,
you say, and go around thinking you're entitled to hurt
people.'

'Hey, they're harsh words!' Matt protested, pulling up
with a jolt outside her building.

'But true!' she told him. 'And as well as hurting other people, you're hurting yourselves. You're stunting your growth—your emotional growth—like a little kid afraid to tackle something new, saying it's too hard. It's not because it's too hard, it's because you're afraid you'll fail—and Phillipses don't fail. Except at relationships, and you excuse yourself about that before you even go into them.'

Matt leaned across and touched her lightly on the arm. 'Have you told Josh all this?'

Kirsten was startled.

'No!'

'Why not?' Matt asked. 'Fear of failure?'

Her heart stood still, but she forced herself to think.

'Probably,' she admitted, then she leaned over and kissed him on the cheek. 'But you're younger, so there's hope for you. Forget the past and look towards the future—be the Phillips who proves he can be a good husband and father.'

Kirsten didn't ask him in, assured him she could cross the footpath and go up in the lift with no risks and thanked him for all he'd done. He sat in the car, waiting until she was safely inside, but her mind wasn't on the younger Phillips male, but the older one. The one she'd be seeing tomorrow.

And she began to think about what Matt had asked—about her own fear of failure.

But I'm a Collins, and Collinses never fail, she told herself as the lift took her up to the fourth floor.

A light shone under Gabi's door and, knowing Alex was still away, she knocked quietly.

'Hi. Good night?' Gabi said, when she'd peered through the peep-hole then opened the door.

'Great,' Kirsten said, but didn't elaborate. 'Look, I'm

sorry to bother you so late, but I know Alex has a toolbox. Would he by any chance have a bit of sandpaper I could borrow?'

'Sandpaper?'

'Sandpaper.'

Gabi shook her head, shrugged, then trotted off, returning a little later with a square of sandpaper.

'You're not going to tell me why you need it, are you?' she said, and Kirsten smiled at her.

'No!'

Then she kissed Gabi on the cheek as she'd kissed Matt, said goodnight and crossed the foyer to her own door.

It was one minute past midday when Kirsten studied the button at the security door outside Josh's building. Every cell in her body was quivering, though this time with doubt and fear rather than desire. It seemed such a wanton thing to be doing, walking into a man's apartment to start an affair, but instinct told her there was something special between them, if she could just get past those barriers to love he had erected in his mind. This was her one shot, and she was gambling on it working.

Her forefinger hovered over the button, then resolutely pressed. Knowing a camera somewhere above the door would be showing her face up in Josh's apartment, she resisted the temptation to smooth down her hair—or smile inanely.

What if he wasn't at home?

What if he no longer wanted her, and here she was with a bag? Admittedly small and filled with little more than toiletries, spare undies, a change of clothes and a T-shirt or two, but she *was* rather assuming things.

'Kirsten. What a delightful surprise. The door's opening, and it's the seventeenth floor.'

Her breathing had become so awkward she wondered about late onset asthma, but she couldn't worry about that now, because she had to cross this big palm-adorned foyer and get into the lift, all the time remembering seventeen.

With a brain that no longer worked.

Somehow she made it, pressed the right button, then, as the lift doors opened high on seventeen, she saw Josh standing in front of her, the door to his apartment open behind him, so she could also see the river, and across it to the hospital.

Which, all of a sudden, seemed a very long way away.

Did he sense her panic that he took the small bag out of her nerveless fingers, then held her hand very tightly as he led her into the apartment.

'Sit. I'll get us a glass of wine—no, champagne! It has to be champagne.'

His voice was husky. Surely he couldn't be nervous. He was used to this—this was what he did. Affairs with no strings attached. Stringless affairs.

Now he was pressing a glass into her hands, talking all the time, his voice soothing though she had no idea what he was saying.

Then he came and sat beside her, took her untouched glass out of her hand and set it on a side table, then turned her face so he could look into her eyes.

'We don't have to do this, you know. We'll both survive without it. It might be hard at times but, Kirsten, I'm far too fond of you, and need you far too badly as a colleague, to force or even coerce you into something you don't want to do.'

But with his fingers holding her chin, barely touching, barely stroking, yet causing flames of fierce desire to shoot through her body, how could she deny she needed him?

'No,' she said, surprised the word sounded so strong when she was practically boneless with apprehension— well, mostly apprehension. 'I *do* want it. I've even brought some sandpaper.'

Dark eyebrows twitched into a frown, and Kirsten wanted to run her fingers across his forehead to smooth the skin. Was it too early to touch him?

'Sandpaper?' Josh repeated the word in such a disbelieving voice she smiled at him.

'For your bedpost,' she explained. 'I might just be another notch in your bedpost, but while I'm here I want to be the only notch, all right?'

'Oh, Kirsten!' he said, laughing as he gathered her into his arms, laughing as he kissed her, gently at first, then with increasing passion. As night followed day, the fire that had always flared between them soon had them grappling with each other's clothes, and he chuckled once again.

'I'd need a mighty big bedpost to put your notch in.'

After which there was no need for words, or not for a very long time, until pangs of hunger woke Kirsten from an exhausted sleep and she looked around. Somehow they'd made their way into the bedroom, though her recollection of the journey was a bit vague.

And though she knew Josh had made it with her, he wasn't here now.

She slipped out of the bed and into the bathroom, showering quickly because this was all so new and she wasn't certain of the etiquette attached to flings. She pulled on one of the T-shirts she'd brought with her, but nothing else. Stripping off each other's clothes earlier had taken an age—whipping off a T-shirt seemed like a much easier option.

Josh was in the kitchen and must have heard her approach, for he turned, smiled at her, then stepped forward to take her in his arms and kiss her cheek, her neck, her shoulder—

'I've got to eat,' she said, stopping as the nuzzling moved lower and wanting him was now vying with her appetite for food.

'Do you think I hadn't figured that out?' he said. 'Look, the domesticated male, preparing a meal for his lady-love.'

And Kirsten looked, seeing the big wicker tray on the bench behind him, with an array of tempting and exotic nibbles on it.

'Finger food—tactile,' he said, picking up an olive and popping it into Kirsten's mouth, then sighing with appreciation as she licked the salty taste of it from his fingers.

'Keep that up, and it could be hours before you eat,' he warned, then he pulled her close again and she relaxed against him, knowing that so far it hadn't been too hard.

CHAPTER ELEVEN

HARD started at midnight, when the shrilling telephone woke them both.

'I've got to go,' Josh said, shrugging into clothes and leaning over to kiss Kirsten at the same time. 'I'm sor—'

She stopped his lips with a kiss.

'Don't you dare apologise,' she said, then added, 'It's not Jack, is it?' Her heart was beating so hard with fear it was a wonder he heard, but he must have for he shook his head.

'Young Michael McKenna. There's something wrong there.'

He was pulling on socks and must have realised Kirsten was also dressing.

'Stay!' he said. 'Go back to sleep. I'm sorry!'

The full apology that time because she was busy gathering up what she'd need at home.

'Don't you dare say that!' she said, hurrying over to his cupboard and reefing out a couple of his shirts, then searching through his drawers for socks and underwear. 'And I won't stay, I'm coming with you. I'll walk home from the hospital. No, too much to carry, I'll take my car. And I've got some spare clothes for you, so come there if you can get away—look, here's a key. Put it on your keyring. I don't know why you live so far away when you're always going to be woken in the night.'

Josh looked at her. She was wearing a long T-shirt and he suspected nothing else—which caused considerable tightening in his groin. And she was whirling around his bedroom, grabbing bits of clothing and issuing orders, pressing a key into his hand. He doubted whether he'd ever seen a more attractive sight.

'Don't worry about toiletries—there's an all-night chemist across from the hospital. I'll grab some from there and keep them for you in the bathroom,' she told him, and he was tempted to remind her that she hadn't wanted this affair conducted from her flat.

But the seductive thought that with less distance to travel between the hospital and her bed, he'd have longer in said bed with her, made him shut up about that particular embargo.

Kirsten made the journey home alone. And far from feeling let down or neglected, she felt warm and wonderful, though she was concerned about Michael and worried about Josh missing even more sleep than he'd already missed this evening.

She woke early, but not to Josh returning, and wondered if he'd gone home after all. Perhaps he'd be more comfortable there. In fact, there were a thousand reasons why he might have made that choice.

Or he might still be at the hospital! In which case...

She showered and dressed hurriedly. Even if Josh wasn't there, the other young patients were always edgier when one of their number had a crisis, and at those times, diverting them with play and activities became even more important.

Up on the ward, there was no sign of Josh, but she was greeted with relief by nursing staff, tired after a night of trying to maintain calm.

'You're an answer to a prayer,' Desley Miller, the night supervisor, greeted her. 'Michael McKenna deteriorated suddenly during the night and that always means a lot of extra activity which wakes the others, so there are some who've been up most of the night and are high as kites, and others who've just gone back to sleep but will be woken any minute by the wild ones if something isn't done. And at this time of the morning, all the staff are always flat out. Could you do something with that lot over there?'

'That lot over there'—four of the healthier children—were playing what sounded like a cowboys and Indians game from the amount of whooping and hollering going on. Kirsten crossed to where they were playing and was greeted warmly. She suggested, as Michael had been so ill during the night—and she still hadn't found out why or what had happened—they make cards and special pictures for him.

She sorted through a box of craft supplies, removed the sharpest scissors in the box from the grasp of a three-year-old, then set them to cutting and pasting.

'This is kid's stuff,' William, a blasé ten-year-old, muttered.

'Not if you do it properly. Look. Fold the paper this way, then that, so every time he opens the card he sees a different picture.'

It was enough of a challenge to keep the boy interested, and as other mobile children joined them, the competition to produce the best card provided extra momentum. But Kirsten knew it wouldn't last. Overtired as they all undoubtedly were, they'd soon be throwing paste and paper at each other.

'When we finish these we might go on with the story we were writing. The adventure of Ward 6C. William, you were working on pictures on the computer, weren't you? Do you want to go on with that, or help tell the story? I've got my little recorder here. We'll start it again from the beginning—it doesn't matter if it's not quite the same.'

Satisfied they were all going to be busy for a while, Kirsten left them, walking through to the tearoom where she had a locker for both personal and work stuff. It was time she dumped her handbag, and she could get the recorder and a pen and notebook at the same time.

Josh was asleep on the couch, looking most uncomfortable as his head was on one armrest and his feet dangled over the end. She moved quietly past him, opened her locker, shoved her handbag in, found what she wanted and was about to leave the room when she realised just what a great opportunity this was.

To look at him—nothing more—although memories of their love-making did intrude. She set them aside, tucking them away in a special part of her mind to be relived when he was no longer part of her life.

Four weeks, she had. Four weeks to show him all the love she felt for him. And if that didn't work for her— then four weeks to gather memories for a lifetime.

She nodded at the sleeping man, refusing to be saddened by the time restriction—refusing to accept anything that might cast a shadow on this precious time together. Then she returned to the children.

Josh woke and cautiously eased into a sitting position, trying to ignore the complaints of the cricks in his neck and back. His brain was foggy with lack of sleep but somewhere in the fog a little flame of delight was glowing—the kind of flame that had his body stirring.

Kirsten! They'd finally done it—made love.

And it had been every bit as exciting as he'd expected. No, it had been way beyond any possible expectation, as she'd been such a generous, responsive, overwhelmingly wonderful lover.

He glanced at his watch, wondering, as his body had gone beyond stirring and was heading for insistence, if he'd have time to whiz over to her place before he started proper work.

Just to see her, nothing more.

It would give his day the kick-start it needed.

Not until he'd checked Michael, though the child's condition had stabilised and he'd been sleeping an hour ago.

He stood up, washed his face and ran wet fingers through his hair, then walked through the ward, heading for his office where he kept a clean shirt and tie.

The active children, who'd been rioting around the place before he'd gone to sleep, were all gathered around a low table in the play area, but it wasn't until one of the group turned, as if aware of his presence, that he realised the person who'd wrought this miracle had been the red-head he'd been determined not to mess with.

Kirsten smiled, and turned back to her task, which appeared to be holding a small recorder in front of one of the kids. His legs wanted to take him in that direction, but Desley was there, reporting on Michael, and he needed to see the little boy.

And the parents, who'd had an extremely anxious night.

They waited until he'd had a look at the sleeping child, and checked the ten-minute obs on his chart, then followed him out of the room.

'What happened, and why did it happen?' Don McKenna asked.

'You know Michael's treatment has caused what we call neutropenia, where the defensive cells naturally produced in the body are so depleted he's susceptible to any infection.'

Josh paused, knowing he, and most doctors, had a tendency to tell too much too quickly.

'When he came in, it was with a bacterial infection, and we were treating that with antibiotics, but after that, and probably in here unfortunately, he picked up a fungal infection as well.'

He paused again and sighed, opting for honesty.

'Actually, I'm guessing that's what happened. He'd been stable then suddenly his temperature shot up, but rather than do tests for a specific infection, I put him straight onto different antibiotics, which attack a variety of fungi. By dripping them into him, we were able to use a high dosage, and going by the fact that his temperature has dropped and his blood pressure is back near normal, I'd say they're already working.'

'But you didn't go home,' Shelley McKenna said, and Josh felt like thumping his forehead.

'I'm sorry. I should have realised that might bother you. I wasn't certain enough to go home. If the antibiotics hadn't worked I'd have had to look for something else.'

He tried a smile but knew it wasn't a particularly good one.

'I know that sounds as if it's all a bit hit and miss, and to a certain extent it is, but it's the only way we know. Kids are so individual, you can't make blanket statements about what will and won't work, and you certainly don't have time to wait for lab results, so—'

'So you sleep on that terrible two-seater in the tea-room,' Shelley finished for him, then offered him a slightly teary smile. 'Next time, kick me out of my bed in Michael's room and sleep there. I'll take the couch.'

Don held out his hand.

'Thanks,' he said. 'And while it did worry us that you stayed, it also made us feel good that you were here.'

Josh made his way to his office where he turned on the urn for coffee, pulled a clean business shirt and tie out of his cupboard, then rubbed his fingers across his chin and crossed to his desk for his electric razor.

Michael was getting better. Young Jack had slept through the night for the first time since his X-ray treatment had started. If everything continued to go well, tomorrow they'd harvest the bone marrow from his sister and start infusing it.

All in all, his life was in order.

He grinned inanely to himself.

Very much in order now he'd got the redhead into his bed.

The grin faded as he realised how much he wanted her there again, and how impossible it was to plan when that might be. Experience had proved that.

Though with her flat just down the road...

He rubbed his razor over his chin, and knew he was more relaxed than he'd been for ages—and that was from just *thinking* about the redhead.

Three weeks and four days later, Josh was still thinking about the redhead.

Constantly!

Today he was shaving again, not because he'd been up most of the night, but because they were going on a real date—to dinner at The Blue Room! He stood at the window of his office and looked out across the city.

Considering the hours they were both working—as well as putting the ward story onto the computer and printing out copies for the young patients, Kirsten was learning how to set up individual videos for the other patients—it was amazing they ever managed to find time to spend together, but they did.

He'd almost ceased being surprised when he'd arrive home after a late meeting, on a night when they'd agreed not to see each other, to find her dozing on his couch, or in his kitchen preparing a snack so he wouldn't go to bed hungry.

'Except for me,' she might add, with a smile that made his toes curl.

Or if he'd stayed at her place, he'd wake, later than he'd intended, to find her dining chairs lined up with all his clothes laid out in the order in which he dressed, the line leading him to the kitchen where a glass of freshly squeezed orange juice might nestle in a bowl of ice, while a plate of easy-to-eat snacks, covered with plastic wrap, stood beside it.

'You needed to sleep and I knew you had nothing special on,' she'd explained, when he'd cornered her later on the ward on that particular day. 'I came early and would have phoned you if there'd been anything untoward happening.'

And cornering her on the ward hadn't been easy. At work she'd been as professional as he always was—in fact, she'd been far more professional than he was, refusing to fall for his little ploys of an occasional 'meeting' in his office. If anyone on the ward suspected they were having an affair, it wasn't because Kirsten had given anything away.

And her inventiveness had led him to think in different ways, working out what might be special for her, whisking her off to a picnic at the beach, a wicker basket of delicious snacks specially prepared for him by Mavis in the coffee-shop. Then, last weekend, with all his patients—even young Jack—stable, they'd sneaked away for a whole two days together, heading for a mountain resort where the beauties of nature had gone largely unappreciated as they'd revelled in the beauty of each other.

At least, he assumed Kirsten found him as beautiful as he found her! For a woman not afraid to voice her opinion on just about any subject under the sun, she wasn't particularly communicative about their relationship.

He finished shaving and rubbed his hand across his chin.

Did lack of comment on it mean she wasn't as fulfilled by the affair as he was?

The thought sneaked beneath his guard, jabbing pain into his intestines.

'No, of course she is. Why else would she be so happy? Such delightful company? Do so much for you?'

Even spoken out loud, the assurances didn't do much for his fast-waning confidence, but when she came to the door of her flat a little later, her smile was so genuine, her delight so obvious, Josh told himself everything was fine.

Until they started on their sweets, and with an 'Oh! Taste this! It's practically orgasmic it's so good!' she offered him a spoonful of her dessert.

Her spoon was between his lips and he was savouring not only the sublime taste but the fact that she was feeding him when she added, in as casual a tone as if the subject were still food, 'You realise our four weeks is up on Sunday. Should we do something special on Saturday night by way of a farewell?'

Naturally, Josh choked on the chocolate ice confection, and though he told her that hitting someone on the back didn't help with choking, she hit him anyway, then made him drink a glass of water, so he wasn't at his best—in fact, his eyes were watering from the choking—when he finally gathered enough wits to tackle the remark that had caused all the trouble.

'Farewell?' He only managed one word—and that hoarsely.

'The end of the fling. Goodbye to four fabulous weeks of sex. If it was a movie, they'd probably call it *The End of the Affair*.'

He tried to concentrate on the issue at stake here—no more Kirsten? But found himself wondering instead if her hair appeared more red this evening.

'We did settle on four weeks, didn't we?' the irritating witch continued. Definitely more red! 'I know you were pretty vague and, as I recall, six weeks got a mention, but I think four weeks was the consensus we reached.'

'*We* did nothing of the kind!' he said, gathering strength from a kind of panic-driven anger now building in his gut. 'You're the one who prattled on about how long my relationships lasted. *I* said it wasn't an issue.'

Kirsten frowned as if trying to recall the conversation, which, damn it all, wasn't the point.

Josh frowned right back at her, then realised frowning wasn't good. Tried a smile instead.

'No matter what we said, there's no reason it can't go on, is there? Unless you're sick of it? Unless you've had enough?'

A cold emptiness in the region of his heart had him praying that wasn't so.

She returned his smile, which allayed a smidgen of his panic. Smiles were good, weren't they?

Then she reached across the table and took his hand.

Even better—these days touching led inevitably to intimacy where he and Kirsten were concerned.

He looked into the green eyes, thinking bedroom, but what he saw there wasn't the sparkle of a sexual invitation but a depth of sadness so obvious it hit him like a fist to the chin.

'I'd never have enough,' she said quietly. 'Which is why it's finishing on Sunday. It's not your fault, Josh. I went into this knowing your rules about relationships, not expecting anything more than a month of unadulterated bliss because I'd be with you. And I've had that and loved every tortured moment of it.'

He wasn't quite following but that last bit sounded hopeful, although he'd have to think about the 'tortured' part later.

'Then why stop? Why can't we just keep going?'

She gave a funny little smile which he guessed was aimed at herself, not him.

'Because I love you, you dope, and because of that it's going to be hard enough leaving you now. If we go on— for what? Three months? A year? Then it will be even harder. And I don't think that would happen. I think we've got enough going for us that we'd go on for about ten years, give or take a year, then one day you'd wake up and decide you were ready for a family. You were born to be a father, so don't deny it to someone who sees you with kids every day. And when that day arrives it would be goodbye, Kirsten, hello much younger woman with good child-bearing hips.'

'You can't honestly believe that!' Josh gasped, the gasp caused more by this rendition of his own logical but never uttered plan than by the actual summing up.

'Don't you?' she asked. 'Hasn't that always been the plan? Your plan?'

He tried to find words to deny it, certain he'd never mentioned this to anyone, but the words wouldn't come. Mainly because there were no words.

This woman had inveigled herself into his life—well,

OK, so he'd done a bit of inveigling, too—and was now calmly walking out on all they had.

And he was hurting.

Maybe choking on the ice cream had ruptured something.

'Look, I'll take you home. We'll talk there.'

'Will we?' she said, but she didn't argue. Which in itself should have warned him. She wasn't usually the non-arguing type, his redhead.

'Home' tonight was his flat, and although their love-making seemed to have a touch extra in the mind-blowing department, nothing more was said. He woke in the morning to find Kirsten gone, but a note explained she had a lot to do back at her flat because she was hosting a baby shower—whatever that might be—for a fellow OT at her flat that night.

As he dressed for work, he tried to think of something special they could do on Saturday night. *Not* because it would be their last night together—that had been a minor aberration in the smooth running of their love life, nothing more—but because she was special and he wanted to let her know.

'So, how about we go to the new show at the Casino on Saturday night?' he said, tracking her down in the canteen and dawdling by the counter until Alana, who'd looked as if she'd been about to leave, stood up and walked away.

Kirsten looked up, not surprised to find him there because she'd been avoiding him all morning and Josh usually got his way.

'I don't think I'll bother,' she said, careful to keep the quavery note of despair out of her voice.

'Won't bother with the Casino?'

He was looking at her with that slightly puzzled expression his face had worn since last night at dinner.

'Won't bother going out. I mean, it was a stupid idea anyway, celebrating the end of the affair.'

'But I wasn't thinking of celebrating the end, just celebrating. We're not going to end. I thought we fixed that up.'

'By talking about it after we left the restaurant? I can't recall much conversation after that—or none that could be included in anything other than an X-rated film.'

She saw the colour creep under his skin and knew it was anger, not embarrassment.

'You're being stubborn, Kirsten. You know damn well we didn't set a time limit on this relationship.'

'No?' She raised her eyebrows, then relented. 'Maybe you didn't, but I did. I decided four weeks would be long enough.' She glanced at her watch and pretended to look startled. 'And look at us, didn't even make it that far.'

'Kirsten—'

'No.'

She'd have liked to have covered her ears with her hands in case he didn't get the message, but didn't want to make it obvious to any interested onlookers that this conversation might be about more than work.

Josh said nothing more, simply studying her face, the blue eyes sweeping across it as if trying to see a crack in her defences.

Heaven knew, there were enough of them, she just had to hope none were showing.

'OK!' he said, and he pushed his still full cup away, stood up and walked away.

'I left my cardigan and our ward is like an ice-box at the moment.'

Alana must have been almost at the table as Josh left,

Kirsten realised, although she hadn't heard her friend approaching.

'If you can hear a cracking noise, it's my heart breaking,' she said to Alana, then with a sigh so deep it must have started in her toes she stood up. 'Come on, let's get the afternoon over and done with, then go home and check out the internet dating agencies. No, tomorrow we'll do that. Tonight I've got the baby shower. You *are* coming?'

Alana put her arm around Kirsten's shoulders and gave her a quick hug. But mercifully she stayed silent, perhaps guessing that one word could have had Kirsten dissolving into tears.

Josh found himself back up on the ward, but had no clear idea of how he'd got there. He had his first student round of the year in half an hour, and wanted to see all the patients first to check if there was anyone who'd be destabilised by a horde of nervous young visitors.

'Young Adam Stokes won't understand,' Betty said, when he found her in a scrub room and put this problem to her. 'I mean, he'll understand enough to know there are a lot of strangers in his room, but telling him why they're there would probably only confuse him.'

Adam was five, but Down's syndrome had delayed his mental development and, according to Kirsten, he was functioning at about the level of a three-year-old. Which, again according to Kirsten—he didn't think he'd ever be able to get her out of his mind—was very good.

But leukaemia was more common in children with Down's syndrome, especially boys, than in the general population, so the students should meet the little boy.

'I'll go and see him, try to explain,' he said. 'I'd hate him to be frightened, or feel invaded by this group.'

Betty nodded, then assured him that all the other patients presently on the ward were stable and in good spirits so, with no further problems, he headed for Adam's room.

To find it already invaded.

Kirsten was there, with Adam's baby brother in her arms. From the look of things, she was doing counting exercises with Adam, using the baby's toes as counters.

Adam was joining in and laughing in delight, but it wasn't the sight of the little boy's laughter that caused the terrifying tightening in Josh's chest. It was the sight of the laughing redhead with the baby in her arms. And suddenly he knew he wanted it—wanted the lot. The redhead, the baby—her baby, hers and his—marriage, everything!

All the stuff he'd been denying wanting for years.

All the stuff he'd been so pragmatic about until she'd out-pragmatised him, offered him four weeks of her life, given him a taste of bliss, then said that was it.

He glared at her as if it was her fault this sudden revelation was so badly timed, but she was too busy playing with Adam and the baby to even notice. Too busy, or simply not aware of him—having wiped him from her mind as easily as one erased from a whiteboard.

Now despair joined the turmoil in Josh's chest because, even if he could, by some miracle, change her mind— after all, she *had* said she loved him—how would it feel to have it all—the redhead, the baby, the whole family scene—then lose it through the Phillips curse?

Which was always putting work first.

And not committing to marriage.

He spoke to Adam's parents, then, as Kirsten moved away, still holding the baby, he talked to the little boy himself, explaining about the other people who'd be coming and who would like to talk to him. At some stage, Kirsten handed the baby back to Mrs Stokes and left the room, but apart from a seeming loss of warmth, he barely noticed.

Any more than he noticed much else that went on during the afternoon, though as no one commented on his behaviour, he must have been acting OK. A night's sleep brought no startling revelations, and by early Saturday afternoon he was so stressed—and his flat so empty—he drove out to see his mother.

'Problems?'

Her greeting left a lot to be desired, so he scowled and muttered, 'Why should there be?'

'You look like a man who hasn't slept for a week, and you're never cranky with your mother unless you're really out of sorts.'

He had to smile.

'Out of sorts doesn't begin to describe it,' he admitted. He sat down at the kitchen table, the very same table where she'd once explained the facts of life, and watched her fill the kettle and fuss about getting out cups, coffee, biscuits.

'I know I don't know everything—actually, I don't know anything—about your and Dad's relationship, but from my viewpoint you can't have given him a reason to leave you.'

His mother continued to prepare the snack as though he discussed her love life every day.

'It wasn't so much that he left me as that I was never really there,' she said, pushing the shortbread aside to make room on the plate for chocolate brownies. 'Work occupied ninety per cent of his time and about the same percentage of his emotions. He had very little left for anything else—or that's how he saw it, anyway.'

She turned and put the plate on the table in front of him.

'It's how I saw it, too,' she admitted. 'You know I was a nurse. I'd worked with his father. I knew that's how your grandfather lived, with his life divided into two compartments—the big one work, a smaller one for family. I think now it was because your father didn't know his own father that he had no idea how to be a father to you boys, so it was easier for him to be busy at work than to try.'

Josh took a brownie, bit into it, and the flooding taste of chocolate in his mouth reminded him of Thursday night—of Kirsten's dessert.

Of Kirsten.

'And we're in the same boat, aren't we? Dad's three sons?' Disturbed by the intrusion of the redhead into his mind when he was trying to remain calm and work things out rationally, he growled the questions at his mother. 'Not having seen a father in action, we're no good at it. Look at Harry and Brad. Both their marriages are in trouble.'

'Both their marriages are in trouble because they don't care. They didn't choose women they loved but women they deemed suitable, so, yes, to a certain extent they were reliving their father's life.'

'Only to a certain extent?' Josh queried as something in his mother's voice sparked an interest beyond his own all but overwhelming concerns.

'In both their cases, the women knew that's how it was. I made sure of that if I did nothing else for them.' She shrugged and he saw her blink away a tear. 'I married your father for love—that was my mistake. And I knew he didn't want it, so I hid it from him, but I always hoped he'd wake up one day and realise he loved me, and then I could tell him.'

She gave a little huff of laughter and added, 'Some dream, huh? What he woke up and realised was that short-term affairs were far more interesting than going home to the wife and kids—it's why we lived out here and he lived in town. While I was accepting this dedication to work, he'd cut it back to about eighty per cent of his time, giving him ten per cent for other diversions. And I'd never have known if one of them hadn't also fallen in love with him, and instead of going quietly when he said it was over, she came out here and told me all about it. She was so young and lovely—she had red hair—I couldn't blame her for what had happened, especially as he was no more in love with her than he was with me.'

Josh sat there, staring at her, hearing the echoes of the pain she must have felt, while some gremlin inside him tied his intestines into knots.

'So what do I do? Forget marriage altogether because of inbred inability to make it work? Stick to my convictions and wait until I'm forty when I'll have time to devote to a family?'

His mother smiled.

'Or marry for love? Haven't you considered that? Isn't it why you're here?'

He should have been shocked—or at least surprised—by her perception, but he was too busy considering this bizarre idea—marry for love—from someone as practical as his mother.

'But Phillips marriages never work,' he protested.

'Only because they never get a chance. Because love never gets a chance. The pig-headed Phillips men go into marriage as if it's one of their own prescriptions—take one woman before bed every night. They won't give love a go. Anyway, it's only one-sided love that founders. Find someone you love, someone who loves you back, and let the strength of that combined love help you make it work.'

'But I'm half yours and you gave it a go,' he reminded her, sure the answer couldn't be that simple. 'And it didn't work for you.'

She flapped her hands at him.

'Get out of here. I've told you what you wanted to hear—told you all I'm going to. From here on in, it's up to you. Just keep in mind one thing—well three things, I suppose. You're not your father, or Brad, or Harry. You're Josh, and at the risk of giving you a swelled head, you're also the most loving and affectionate of all my children. It's what makes you such a good paediatrician. And will make you a wonderful husband and a totally besotted father.'

Even though the words were certainly encouraging, he still hesitated, gripped by fear now instead of doubts.

'We might have had this talk too late. I might have lost her,' he admitted as his mother scooped away his cup and turned to the sink to rinse it out.

'If you're talking about Kirsten, I doubt it,' she said, looking out across the fields towards the creek.

'How do you know about Kirsten?' he demanded, standing up and moving closer as if up close he might be able to detect her witchcraft.

'I met her at the Bush Dance, only she was Dolly then and engaged to someone else. Then you took me the to The Blue Room and when we joined her and Matt I realised why. After that I phoned her and asked her out to visit me. She came last weekend. Sunday afternoon. You had that paper to prepare so she was at a loose end and—'

'Stop this conversation right now, and go back to the bit about The Blue Room!' Josh growled. 'You realised why what? Or what why?'

'That she was the woman you wanted—the one you've been pining over for the last I don't know how long.' She paused then corrected herself. 'Actually, I do know how long. A bit over a year—Kirsten told me.'

'You and Kirsten have been discussing me behind my back?' Forget love, he was practically incoherent with rage, and getting madder by the minute. His father had been right about redheads, only he shouldn't have stopped at them! Don't mess with women, he should have said, and included his mother—wife—whatever—in the embargo!

'Oh, no. She wouldn't do that. She just explained about how things started between you, then stopped, then started again.'

'And stopped!' Josh roared. 'Did she tell you that part? Tell you it was stopping again—has, in fact, stopped?'

His mother looked puzzled, which wasn't surprising as he'd never yelled at her before. Then she turned and looked out the window again.

'No, she didn't tell me that,' she said, shaking her head as if the scene before her was somehow puzzling. 'Although I did think it was a bit odd when she came by this morning to ask about camping and said something about wanting to feel close to you.'

The gremlins had departed from his abdomen, leaving everything nicely knotted, and were now dancing, in hobnailed boots, around his brain, stirring what had once passed for usable cells into total confusion.

'Camping to feel close to me?'

His mother nodded to the window.

'Down by the creek. She's camping there—in that little glade.'

'In *my* glade?'

Now his mother faced him.

'Well, I didn't know you'd taken it as yours, but you know the one.'

'What's she doing there? And don't say camping! I'm still angry.'

'Why don't you ask her?'

For a split second he considered walking away—getting into his car and driving back to the city. But that's what his father would have done—had done—and, as his mother had just pointed out, he wasn't his father.

He gave his mother a quick hug by way of apology for yelling, then walked down to the creek, turning left along the path leading into the glade. The small tent was pitched at the far side so it almost melted into the bushes, but it was the woman sitting by the creek, her feet dangling in the water, who drew his attention.

'What are you doing here?' he demanded, and saw the flash of red as a straying sunbeam caught her hair.

'Camping,' she said, her voice as smooth as silk, her face expressionless.

Cute! She was going to be cute! Well, he could be cuter. No way would he ask the obvious.

'In *my* glade?' he said instead—after all, who was she to dispute the ownership?

'Well, I think of it more as Michael's glade,' Kirsten said, looking around then lifting her hand as if to catch the sunbeam. 'You must really have had an incredible empathy with him to help him find this place in his head, and for him to be able to draw it so accurately. It's when I first realised that, no matter how hard you might fight it, you're actually perfect father material.'

Something squished inside Josh's knotted intestines.

'So the four weeks were bait, were they? Enough time to trap me into marriage? Are you pregnant?'

She looked startled, then laughed.

'Hey, who was the one who insisted on condoms?' she

said. 'Every single time, no matter where we were? Me, that's who.'

She stood up then and crossed the glade towards him, and he wanted to warn her there might be prickles in the grass, but his mouth had gone dry.

She took his hands in hers then leaned forward and kissed him on his frozen lips.

'But let's not waste our time together. Want to make love in my tent? Or on the grass? I've got a blanket. And condoms.'

He felt his lips moving but no sounds were coming out, so he tried harder, concentrated, thought things through.

'The four weeks are up,' he finally managed, then realised that was the last thing he should have said. He shouldn't have mentioned it—shouldn't have reminded her!

But she seemed unfazed, simply smiling then tugging as if to lead him to the tent.

He didn't move, so she turned back and snuggled close to his chest, lifting lips so luscious it was a wonder a man didn't go mad, looking at them.

'Not until tomorrow,' she murmured, then sealed the words with a kiss.

The kind of kiss that weakened his knees, so soon they were on the grass, sitting and then lying—no blanket, and probably there'd be prickles.

Josh was almost at the point of no return when the words 'not until tomorrow' finally registered in his bewildered brain. He sat up, hastily snapping closed the studs on his jeans.

'What do you mean, not until tomorrow? You're not going to make love to me here in my glade today then tell me tomorrow it's all over?'

The green eyes opened so wide he thought he might fall into them and drown.

'Don't you want it to be over?' she asked, all innocence, but he wasn't buying it.

'Of course I don't want it to be over,' he grumbled. 'You know I don't.'

Kirsten smiled the kind of smile he knew boded ill for anyone in her vicinity—and guess who that was?

'I suppose we could organise a new contract,' she said, her voice so sultry and seductive he wished he hadn't snapped all the studs on his jeans as they were now becoming uncomfortably tight. 'Another four weeks?'

In another four weeks she was going to put him through this again?'

'No!'

The smiled widened.

'Shorter or longer?' she asked, the tiny freckles practically sparkling with delight as she teased him.

But the question had merit, and though he knew the answer—it was definitely longer—he also knew what her next question would be—how much longer? And that was the one to make him stop and think.

'Well?'

Was the voice now not so certain? Were the green eyes clouded with a hint of doubt?

And suddenly Josh didn't want her doubting or uncertain. Didn't want to cause her a moment's pain, though he knew he probably would, some time in the future.

But for now it was enough to gather her into his arms, pulling her onto his knee and holding her close.

'How does for ever sound to you?' he whispered, pushing the heavy fall of hair aside so he could nuzzle her ear as he spoke. 'For ever and ever, in sickness and health, and all that mushy wedding stuff—but you and I, when *we* say it, we'll mean it. Or at least I will.'

He eased her back so he could look at her face—so she could look at him as well.

'Will you? For ever?'

Kirsten nodded, and tears welled up in her eyes, and because he couldn't bear to see his redhead cry, he drew her close again and kissed the tears away.

From her eyelids, then her cheeks, her lips, and right on down her neck. He ran out of excuses after that but kissed other bits of her anyway, in celebration of the great event. A Phillips committing to marriage and meaning it in the true sense of the word—commitment!

Modern Romance™
...seduction and
passion guaranteed

Tender Romance™
...love affairs that
last a lifetime

Sensual Romance™
...sassy, sexy and
seductive

Blaze Romance™
...the temperature's
rising

Medical Romance™
...medical drama on
the pulse

Historical Romance™
...rich, vivid and
passionate

27 new titles every month.

*With all kinds of Romance for
every kind of mood...*

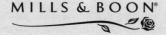

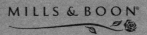

Medical Romance™

THE DOCTOR'S DESTINY *by Meredith Webber*

Dr Rory Forrester thought he knew better than Nurse Alana Wright – yet she found him incredibly attractive! They might be colleagues in conflict, but the chemistry between them was intense. Rory realised he had found an angel who could answer his prayers – but one thing stood in their way...

THE SURGEON'S PROPOSAL *by Lilian Darcy*

Theatre sister Annabelle Drew was shattered when one of her guests uttered 'Stop the wedding' as she was about to say 'I do'! But surgeon Dylan Calford had no regrets – until he discovered how badly Annabelle had needed her marriage of convenience. So he proposed that he should be her groom instead...

UNDER SPECIAL CARE *by Laura MacDonald*

Mutual attraction flared between Sister Louise Keating and Dr Matt Forrester, and a whirlwind marriage followed. But finding time for each other proved impossible, and they separated. Now, a year on, they're working together again, in the special care baby unit. As they heal their tiny patients, can they also heal their marriage...?

On sale 7th March 2003

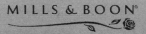

MILLS & BOON®

Medical Romance™

THE DOCTOR'S GIFT by Lucy Clark

When locum Dr Kelly O'Shea roars into the small Australian village, Dr Matt Bentley's heart flips. But he has been burned by love and intends to keep away. Yet their sizzling attraction culminates in an earth-shattering kiss — and Kelly has to admit her secret. She's pregnant with her ex-husband's child!

EMERGENCY AT BAYSIDE by Carol Marinelli

Emergency sister Meg O'Sullivan has come to Bayside Hospital to start afresh. But, tired and dazed after a traumatic day, she finds herself upside down in her car. Dr Flynn Kelsey risks his own life to save her, and they discover they are colleagues. Their attraction is explosive — and then Meg sees a photo of Flynn's wedding...

DATING DR CARTER by Judy Campbell

Dr Iona Bellamy has spent three years trying to get charismatic Matt Carter — the ultimate playboy doctor — out of her system. Then he reappears — as her new boss! Working under temptation drives their passions to reignite — until Iona hears Matt's father offering him half a million pounds to walk down the aisle...

On sale 7th March 2003

FREE!

2 Books
and a surprise gift!

We would like to take this opportunity to thank you for reading this Mills & Boon® book by offering you the chance to take TWO more specially selected titles from the Medical Romance™ series absolutely FREE! We're also making this offer to introduce you to the benefits of the Reader Service™ —

- ★ FREE home delivery
- ★ FREE gifts and competitions
- ★ FREE monthly Newsletter
- ★ Books available before they're in the shops
- ★ Exclusive Reader Service discount

Accepting these FREE books and gift places you under no obligation to buy; you may cancel at any time, even after receiving your free shipment. Simply complete your details below and return the entire page to the address below. *You don't even need a stamp!*

YES! Please send me 2 free Medical Romance books and a surprise gift. I understand that unless you hear from me, I will receive 4 superb new titles every month for just £2.55 each, postage and packing free. I am under no obligation to purchase any books and may cancel my subscription at any time. The free books and gift will be mine to keep in any case.

M3ZEB

Ms/Mrs/Miss/Mr ....Initials...
BLOCK CAPITALS PLEASE

Surname...

Address...

....

....Postcode ....

Send this whole page to:
UK: The Reader Service, FREEPOST CN81, Croydon, CR9 3WZ
EIRE: The Reader Service, PO Box 4546, Kilcock, County Kildare (stamp required)

Offer not valid to current Reader Service subscribers to this series. We reserve the right to refuse an application and applicants must be aged 18 years or over. Only one application per household. Terms and prices subject to change without notice. Offer expires 30th May 2003. As a result of this application, you may receive offers from Harlequin Mills & Boon and other carefully selected companies. If you would prefer not to share in this opportunity please write to The Data Manager at the address above.

Mills & Boon® is a registered trademark owned by Harlequin Mills & Boon Limited.
Medical Romance™ is being used as a trademark.